The Dragon King

Katimeana Keloy

Special thanks to:

The original cast of The Dragon King. I never could have made this without you.

Shante, you've been a great help and inspiration. I will never forget the unless nights we spent coming up with ideas.

Prologue

The sky was dark. It had started to rain. People began to leave to find shelter from the coming storm. There was heartbreak in the air. Everyone could feel it. The few who were left looked down at the freshly covered grave. A loved one had moved on.

A woman in long black robes mumbled a few words before turning to follow the rest of the crowd back toward the center of the small town in which they lived. She was particularly troubled; the recently deceased had been her brother. She stared at the name etched into the stone: JAMES ALEXANDER RYNNE, and tried to convince herself that he was in a better place. Unable to hold it back any longer, she bursts into tears. Her husband put his arm around her and ushered her back home.

Slowly the rest of the people departed, until only one was left. A small boy, also dressed in black. A poor boy who had just lost his father. He held a single red rose in his grubby little hands. Tears mixed with the rain that streamed down his face as he knelt down in the mud next to the final resting place of his father. Carefully, he laid the rose down on top of the grave.

"Axel!" A woman's voice called. The child turned, and looked up to see his mother beckoning him to come. She was already a good distance away, and it was hard to hear her over the sound of the growing winds. The wind blew her hood off her head, exposing her long, brown hair to the elements. Her face was quite beautiful, and her cheeks were rosy red from the cold. As the growling wind whipped her hair behind her, her long black dress and long bell sleeves flapped ferociously as if trying to get away from her. "Axel, there's a great storm coming. Come, and let us get home quickly."

The boy rose to his feet, and turned to take one final look at the spot where he'd last seen his father's face. The rose was gone. It had been swept away by the wind. He looked around for it frantically, but it was nowhere in sight.

"Axel!" The boy's mother called him again, coming closer. Worry was etched into her face as she watched her son ignore her and continue to search for the lost flower. Axel was determined to find that rose. His mother quickened her pace, following after her son as he searched intently for the flower.

A young girl stood behind her, trying her best to keep up with her. Lighting flared across the sky, making her scream out in terror. Axel's mother turned, and the girl clung to her legs. She was only three years old, just two years younger than Axel. "Krystal, did I not tell you to follow the others home?" The woman sighed as she picked up her youngest child and held her close to her. She had started to cry and so her mother tried to comfort her while still keeping an eye on Axel.

"The rose for father is gone!" The boy cried, still ignoring his mother. His eyes sped over every inch of the earth before him as he continued his search.

"Let us get another one tomorrow, darling." His mother said, finally reaching him and putting a hand on his shoulder.

He shoved her hand away and kept searching. "No! I picked that rose particularly for Father! I must find it!"

"Axel, please." His mother said, shifting the girl on her hip to the other side, "Your father cared more for your health than the gift that you gave to him. Come, let us return home."

Axel continued to ignore his mother.

Thunder crashed and Krystal screamed out again, burying her face into her mother's chest. Everyone was so soaked already that her tears on her mother's clothes did not make any difference. Their mother thought about the situation a moment. How could she successfully get her son to safety without depriving him of a chance to say goodbye to his father? She looked up at the dark sky, and at the black clouds that swirled in the air above them. The storm was getting worse, and Krystal was getting more and more uncontrollable every time thunder sounded and she became more frightened. "Axel," she said at long last, getting an idea, "Your father is a part of the spirits now. The wind was only helping to deliver your present directly up to him." She smiled down at her son, and at her own cleverness.

His bright blue eyes glistening with tears, the boy stopped his search momentarily to look up into his mother's dark brown eyes. "Really?"

"Yes, my son." She said, ushering him along. He held out his arms for her to pick him up. She sighed, and carefully bent down to pick him up and place him on her other hip. "Let us hurry before Father sees us outside." As quickly as she could, she carried her two youngest children to the shelter of their small home.

Chapter One

  Rebecca stood out on her terrace overlooking the small town of Salbris. She was a rich girl, or at least her father was, and she had almost everything she ever wanted. There was only one thing that she longed for that money could not buy her, and that was love. Not just any love, of course she had the love of her parents, and sometimes her brother, but she wanted the love of a man. A man to call her own, a husband. She wasn't about to just settle for anyone either. She had already picked him out, all she had to do was convince him that she was the right one for him. She could see his little farm from her terrace, and loved to just sit and watch everything that went on there. She liked to watch him as he came out to give water to the cows, his beautiful muscles bulging with the weight of the bucket, and imagined how wonderful it would feel with those gorgeous arms of his wrapped around her. He would also milk the cows, and plough the fields, and take care of the other animals. Sure, his brothers helped too, but she barely noticed them. Sometimes she would see him talking with his sister or with a few of his friends, but he really spent most of his time working. He always seemed to be busy doing something. Heaven knows he was always too busy to talk to her. She had tried several times to get his attention, but nothing seemed to work. She just needed to know what kind of girl he wanted. Then she would conform herself to that lifestyle. She didn't care what it took. She would do anything for him.

  Just then, the door to his little peasant home opened up, and she saw a glimpse of his glorious face. His eyes were as blue as the sky, and just as enchanting. His face wasn't real angular like some of the older boys that her mother had introduced her to, but neither was it plump and round. It was a perfect face that Rebecca knew had to have been hand crafted by God himself. His short brown hair flowed ever so slightly in the gentle breeze as he breathed in the fresh morning air.

Rebecca ran from her terrace back into her room where she looked herself over in the mirror. She had already curled her hair, put on one of her best dresses, and done her make-up. Everything had to be perfect before she left to go see her prince. She poofed up her hair, pulled down her dress, and ran out the door.

Once in the hallway she called for her faithful servant Jeremiah. Jeremiah, like his father before him, had served the VanHaughe family his entire life. Since his father died, Jeremiah had been assigned as Rebecca's personal assistant in his place. Which pretty much meant that he had no free will of his own. Despite the fact that they were both the same age, Rebecca never let Jeremiah forget his place. He was the dirt under her shoes. He was no different than a tool to her. Any one of the servants could come and take his place, and it wouldn't matter to her in the least. As long as someone came running when she ordered them to, she would be happy. The only difference between Jeremiah and any of the other servants was that Rebecca actually remembered his name.

Jeremiah was told to make the carriage ready because they were going to town. He sighed and followed his orders. Rebecca was all fancied up and in a hurry to leave - that could only mean one thing. They were going on another pretend trip to the market where she would *just happen* to see Axel and run into his not-so-loving arms. If only their roles were reversed, and she was running to see Jeremiah... Oh, how he would embrace her and never let her go! Will she ever see how much she is missing? Doesn't she notice how Axel cowers away from her and wishes that she was gone? The fool! How could he take her undying love for granted? Jeremiah would give anything to be him just once, and to see her face light up for him, to have her run to him, and love on him. Axel could have it all, and he doesn't care. Every night Jeremiah prayed for the day when Rebecca, too, would realize this.

Despite how much it hurt him inside, Jeremiah shut his mouth, kept his feelings bottled, and went to the stables to fetch his horse. He was, after all, only a servant boy, and that was all she would ever see him as. Rebecca was already waiting impatiently outside the mansion by the time he drove the carriage slowly to the front doors.

"It is about time you got here." She snipped, gathering up her skirts and entering the carriage.

Jeremiah just ignored her and set the carriage into motion. It was only about 5 minutes until they reached the market, and Rebecca didn't even bother to pretend to look around before sprinting off in the direction of the small farm where her beloved Axel lived. His farm was across the street and just a little bit down the road from the market. Jeremiah watched her go, his heart going with her. He broke his eyes away and tied up his horse before having a look around the market.

He had been here enough by now that everyone knew him and he knew everyone there. He walked down the line of market stalls, greeting all the vendors in turn while glancing around to see if there was anything that he did need while he was here. There was John, the fisherman, Peter the butcher, Laura sold candles, Linda made clothes, and several others that sold a variety of produce. Bryam was here today, too, which was a treat because it was only on very rare occasions that he ever really left the house. He was Axel's uncle, and as everyone knew, he had three young boys to do all his farm work now, so he usually just sat at home and reaped in what others had sown. Times, however, were tough, and so Bryam had come to the market to gain a few extra coins.

Despite his large size and ever growing weight, Bryam was a great dancer. He was surprisingly light on his feet and could play the flute and do a little jig at the same time. He had a dirty old cap that he used to collect coins, and so Jeremiah fished his money pouch out of his pocket and threw a few in. Bryam paused long enough to smile and thank him, then continued entertaining the crowd.

Jeremiah was glad to have a well-earned distraction from his ever breaking heart.

Axel was arguing with his mother on his way out the door. She was going on about how he was almost 18 years old and he had never had a girlfriend. He was going to officially be an adult tomorrow and he needed to have a wife. *Blah Blah Blah.* He sighed. His older brother Jarron didn't have a wife and he was 21 years old! Sure, he had a girl that he was courting, and his other brother Westley had just tied the knot last week, but Axel was an independent man, what did he need a wife for? He knew how to take care of himself. Just because he never had a girlfriend, and was now (almost) officially an adult, did not mean he had to get married and immediately start his own family. He just hadn't met the right girl yet, that was all.

Sure he was still living at home for the time being, but that was only because he was helping to take care of his family. Both his brothers were still at home too. Even Westley's new wife, Venessa, lived at their farm. It was a good thing that they had a big farm. Westley would be moving out shortly, though, as soon as they were finished building his new house. Even then, he would only be right down the street from the rest of the family, and able to visit as much (or as little) as he wanted.

Axel's uncle had grown fat and lazy since he taught him and his brothers how to do all the chores. His sisters weren't much by way of help either, they were also lazy and scared to death of a little dirt. They wouldn't go near the pigs, stayed far away from the chickens, and they would never, ever, even think of touching a cow to milk it. Even if their lives depended on it.

"You should get to know the baron's daughter." His mother was saying, "She fancies you, you know."

"I know!" complained Axel. He found the baron's daughter to be quite annoying. Practically every day she came to his house, every time in a different dress, trying, only too obviously, to get his attention. He usually tried his best to ignore her and continue on with whatever it is that he's doing. Sometimes he has to make something up just to get her to leave.

"Look, here she comes now!" His mother said excitedly. "Say something nice to her. Go on, tell her how pretty she looks." She grinned, and hurriedly started to busy herself with hanging the laundry out to dry. Axel went to help her, but she insisted that he go talk to the girl who was now within earshot of what they were saying. Axel rolled his eyes and turned around to face the devil's spawn.

"Axel! How nice to see you, love!" She ran up to him and embraced him in a tight hug before he even had a chance to say hello. She refused to let go for at least five minutes. When he finally wiggled out of her grasp, he backed away from her and smoothed out his shirt.

"Hello, Rebecca." He grunted, in an obviously annoyed monotone voice.

"Axel, my love, how many times must I tell you to call me Becca?" She laughed in her cackling annoying-as-heck way, making Axel want to cringe. He glanced over at his mom, who smiled encouragingly. He sighed.

"Re... Uh, Becca, you look very... uhm... bedizened today." Axel said, trying to fake a smile, which resulted in an odd look that closer resembled a sneer than anything else.

Axel's mother snorted with laughter, then faked a cough to try to cover it up while trying to compose herself.

Rebecca, having no idea what the word "bedizened" actually meant, took it as a compliment and beamed up at Axel with her cheeks blushing. "Why, thank you!" She exclaimed, happy as ever to get more than two words out of Axel for a change. She spun around, happily showing off her dress. Axel turned away from her and tried, unsuccessfully, to make himself look busy. "So Axel, my love, my father is having a grand ball tomorrow night. Everyone of Salbris is invited in welcoming the Duke of Ryonshire to stay with us for a few days during his long journey south. I cannot wait to see you there! You will be in attendance, will you not, Axel?"

"Yes!" Axel's mother practically shouted immediately after Rebecca had finished talking. "I mean, ahem, of course! It's all he talks about. Been planning it for weeks, really."

"Mother!" Axel said, horrified that she was volunteering him for this torturous event.

"It is settled then. You shall be my date for the dance tomorrow. I will see you then, love!"

Quick as lightning, she pecked his cheek with a kiss and then turned and ran off, practically jumping with joy and excitement. Axel sighed and turned to his mother. "Did you really have to do that?"

She giggled in response. She glanced up at the pained look on her son's face and couldn't contain it any longer. She burst out laughing so hard she started to cry.

"I am glad you find this amusing." Axel said, turning to go back inside. He spent the next several hours contemplating how to get out of this disaster his mother had thrown him into. Little did he know that was the last time he would ever see Rebecca VanHaughe alive.

*****

Axel was walking alone down the dusty road that led to the woods at the edge of the town of Salbris. His plain peasant tunic flowed slightly behind him. There was a gentle breeze, but it hardly helped to keep him cool. It was an unusually hot day for it only being the seventh of October, and his face was drenched in sweat. The crinkled piece of parchment in his left hand only added to it. On the piece of paper, someone had scrawled a letter. It was addressed to Axel, and it was signed by The Wizard.

Soon after Axel had finished his chores earlier this morning, a messenger had delivered it to him. It was a short message, saying only to come into the woods at the very center where The Wizard was found. This worried Axel slightly. Seeing The Wizard was not necessarily a good thing. The Wizard was a very mysterious person, and not much was known about him. (Assuming he was a he, seeing as no one that Axel knew had ever actually seen him, he had to be open to the possibility that The Wizard could be female, even though he highly doubted it.) The Wizard was said to have immense powers, able to do whatever he wanted, whenever he wanted to do it. What could he possibly want from Axel? Axel was shocked and confused upon receiving such summons, but on the bright side, it was his birthday today. Although that barely helped to lift his spirits.

Just then, Axel's best friend Conner noticed him quickly making his way down the road. He smiled and waved, but Axel either didn't see him, or just plain ignored him. "Axel!" He called out, running to meet him, "Happy 18th birthday! Hey, where are you headed in such a hurry?"

"Oh, hello, Conner." Axel replied, not stopping even to

look at his friend. "The Wizard has sent for me, so I must leave to find him."

"The Wizard? *The Wizard*, indeed?" Conner exclaimed, excitement growing inside him like wildfire.

"Yes, The Wizard, Conner." Axel was slightly annoyed that Conner was bugging him at this important moment in his life. Not just anyone got called to see The Wizard. You had to be a great warrior, or incredibly important. Usually both. Axel, however, was neither. He was just a poor lowly peasant boy who worked hard every day just to keep his family in good health. This was the first time he had had any communication with anyone who was even slightly more important than the common peasants that he normally hung out with. That is, unless you count Rebecca, which he didn't.

Conner and Axel had known each other for as long as either of them could remember. They didn't really become best friends though until just last year when Conner had graduated from The Academy. He was taller than Axel, and thin, with shoulder-length, curly, brown hair. Conner's hair was his most prized possession (it did match his eyes perfectly, if he did say so himself), and usually what the girls liked best about him. Besides his wonderful personality and great sense of humor, of course. "May I come? Please? I have always wanted to see The Wizard! Very few have ever laid eyes on him. What do you say, Axel?" Conner gave his friend his best puppy dog look.

Axel sighed. "I suppose so. Do not blame me if you are not allowed inside. The Wizard only sent for me."

"Splendid!" Conner said, practically jumping for joy as he took his place at Axel's side. "Is this not exciting? Are you excited, Axel?"

"Yea, yea, splendid indeed." Axel said sarcastically. Axel, in contrast to Conner, was broad-shouldered and well built. He had short, light brown hair, and a neatly trimmed patch of hair on his chin. He was very sarcastic, and easily annoyed. Not that he was a bad person, he was just much more serious than his light-hearted comrade. When he was given a task, he wanted to get it done and over with as quickly as possible, but it also had to be done right. Especially if it was something as serious as going to see The Wizard.

They were traveling east, and had just entered into the great forest. Axel walked forward with a purpose, staring straight ahead and glancing around only to look for any signs that might help them in their search for The Wizard. Conner, however, was so giddy that he couldn't keep still and his head darted around taking in everything around them. As they walked deeper into the forest they noticed that it had grown terribly quiet. Much too quiet. Where were all the animals that lived out in the woods? Why were there no deer? Rabbits? Chipmunks? Where were the birds? The insects? Anything to tell them that they were not alone in this world. Even weirder, there was no wind, no rustle of branches, twigs, or leaves. Not even the grass dared to move in this eerie calm. At one point, Conner stepped on a twig and the sound seemed to echo around the vast nothingness, loud as thunder on a stormy night. Axel wondered for a moment why the sound of the twig snapping in half was amplified while the sound of their feet hitting the ground was not.

After what seemed like hours of walking (or was it days? They lost all sense of time in this strange place), they came upon a dark cave. A wooden sign stuck in the ground in front of the entrance declared, "THE WIZARD".

Axel stopped to stare at the sign and the rather tiny cave. Conner was not convinced. "Are you sure that this is the right place?"

Axel shrugged his shoulders and pointed to the old wooden sign. "It says 'The Wizard', does it not?"

Conner looked around skeptically. There wasn't much too see. They had come to a clearing in the trees, where not even the grass ventured to sprout up. There were no signs of life in this circle of land, just dirt and old rock. Really, anything could be in that cave. What if it was a dragon's lair? Or the home of a dwarf? Or a hungry bear? Or some other wild being that was angry that they were invading its private property...

The sign that Axel pointed to was superannuated. It was cracked and worn, and you could just barely make out the letters that formed the words that were written upon it. Quite possibly it had been put up many years ago as a joke, and no one had ever bothered to take it down. The mighty and powerful Wizard would not live in such an inconsequential insignificant cavern. There was no way. This couldn't be the right place. Still, perhaps they ought to take a look around. Maybe there was another sign telling them what to do next? Or a secret passage that led to where ever The Wizard really was? It may be, perchance, that the next step in their journey lay just inside the darkness of the cave...

Axel moved forward to enter the cave, and just as he was about to cross into the unknown, a loud voice came booming out of its depths, sending him flying backwards and landing on his rump a few feet away.

"WHO ART THOU AND WHY HAST YE COME?"

Axel tried to keep calm as he slowly got to his feet. The thunderous voice left his ears ringing in pain. He had thought the snapping twig was loud. *Ha!* That was nothing compared to the incredibly deep roar he had just apprehended. Axel tried to brace himself for the next blast as he answered feebly, "It is I, Axel. Axel Rynne, sir, sire, uh..." He wasn't quite sure how to address someone as great as The Wizard. "You sent for me."

"I KNOW WHO YE ART. WHO IS IT THAT IS WITH YE?"

"I..." Conner stepped forward a few steps, shaking terribly. "I... I am..." Before he could say anything else, he collapsed to the ground. He was fun and funny, but not very brave.

Axel rolled his eyes. You would think that the loudness of the voice alone would be enough to throw him back into consciousness, but there he lay, in a crumpled heap on the ground, peacefully knocked out at what could be the single most important moment of Axel's young life. "This is my friend, Conner, sir. Conner Kalloway. He is an honorable man and just." Then he added more quietly to himself, "Even if he is not the sharpest sword in the shop."

"THIS IS GOOD. THE BOY SHALL ACCOMPANY YOU ON YOUR JOURNEY."

Axel wanted to say that Conner wasn't a boy, he was 18 years old and already graduated from The Academy and that much alone should qualify him as a man. Axel was not dumb enough, however, to argue with the most powerful being alive. Instead he asked the second thing that came to his mind, "My journey, sire?" What on earth was he talking about? Perhaps this wasn't The Wizard at all. Maybe he was just another messenger to tell them where to go next. Could he be about to show them the way to the place where the real Wizard lived? Axel felt the adrenaline rush through him. This was it. The moment he was waiting for. He was actually going to see The Wizard! If only Conner would wake up! He would be so excited that he would probably faint...

"DOTH THOU NOT WISH TO BE REUNITED WITH THY FATHER?"

"Yes!" Axel answered immediately, although he was shocked by the question. The words echoed around inside his head. Had he heard them right? His father? Wasn't The Wizard supposed to be omniscient? Did he not know that his father had left this earth a very long time ago? Could The Wizard really have the power to raise the dead? Was this "journey" some kind of test to prove his worth? He would do anything for the chance to see his father again. Anything.

"GO." The voice boomed, "LOOK FOR THE BENT TREE LIMB. YOU WILL FIND THERE WHAT IT IS THAT THOU SEEKETH."

"Sire?" Axel asked uncertainly. What was he supposed to do? Which bent tree limb was he to find? He was no great sailor, or a navigator, no, he was nothing but a mere boy! (Well, technically, he was old enough to be a man on his own now, but this was a bit much) Besides, he had no heading, no sense of direction, not a thing to go by! Was he to just wander aimlessly throughout the woods just hoping to eventually one day stumble upon whatever it was that he was supposed to be looking for? What if he never found it? What if-

"GO! QUICKLY NOW, BOY, OR ALL WILL BE LOST!" With that the closing silence engulfed them once more.

"Yes, sir!" Axel called to the now muted, seemingly empty cave. He walked over to Conner and shook him awake. "Wake up, Conner! We must return to the town and prepare for our journey."

"What? How is my hair?" asked Conner, sitting up suddenly. His hands flew to his head where he spent the next several minutes making sure that not a single strand of his beloved hair was out of place.

"Forget your hair! We have to get going." Axel said, already moving in the direction from which they came.

Conner was still sitting on the ground looking dazed and confused. "What? Where are we headed?"

"We are going to find my father." He said, not turning around to look at him. He continued to walk back towards the town. Conner quickly got up and started to follow him.

"Axel, your father is-" Conner was about to say "dead" but a glare from Axel shut him up quick.

"Yes, indeed." He said instead, "Let us go."

*****

Rebecca waited and waited, but her prince charming never showed his face at the ball. Why hadn't she gone to his house earlier to remind him? She had been so busy getting ready that she'd barely even made it in time, and it was in her own house!

She never lost faith that he was coming until there was only an hour left and her hopes began to fall. All night she had thought, *He's just running a little late... He'll be here any minute...* Several times she strode around the grand ball room looking every guest over to make sure she hadn't missed him, but most of the time she stood at the top of the grand staircase, her eyes glued on the great arched doors at the back of the hall, imagining them opening to a great trumpet fanfare and announcing the arrival of the Axel, holder of the key to her heart.

After the initial pouring in of most of the guests, every time a few stragglers came through her heart would skip a beat as she jumped to life ready to tackle him down with hugs and kisses, but alas, every time she was disappointed. When the door had ceased to open again for over two hours, she decided to have a look around to be certain he wasn't already there. She was greeted warmly by several men, some about her age, and others fathers looking to put in a good word for their sons. Rebecca was, after all, the most sought after bachelorette in all of Salbris. She smiled halfheartedly at some, said "hello" dismissively to others, and offended mostly every guy there to be sure. But she didn't care about any of that, nor did she even really realize she was doing it. All she could think about was Axel. By eleven o'clock that night, despair had finally started to wash over her. It came first as worry, wondering if something could have happened to him, but by the end of the night she knew he had just abandoned her. She sat in a chair off to one side of the room and started to cry. Only Jeremiah seemed to notice her.

"Milady," he said, bending down so his face was close to hers. It had taken him all night to build up the courage to say something to her, and he was still scared that she'd reject him. He lifted her chin up gently so that her eyes met his. Even with her eyes red from crying, her makeup ruined, and her hair a mess he still thought she was the most beautiful creature he had ever seen. He took a deep breath, trying to remain cool, calm, and collected. "Would you like to dance?" He sounded much braver than he felt as he stood up and held out his hand for her to take. His heart beat loudly in his chest as he waited for her reply.

At first he thought she was going to reject him. She remained silent and held his gaze, hot tears streaming down her face. He came close again, and held the side of her face in his hand and wiped her cheek with his thumb. For a while he was lost in her ocean blue eyes. Then, as if in slow motion, she rose from her chair, put her hand in his, and laid her head gently on his chest. She then placed her arms around his neck and continued to weep silently. Even with the wetness of her tears sinking through to his skin and her makeup ruining his best white shirt, this was the happiest moment of Jeremiah's young life. Long after the music had stopped playing, Jeremiah and Rebecca stood in the middle of the ballroom, holding each other tight and swaying slightly.

The baron, however, was not too happy with this union. He still saw Jeremiah as property, a thing that was only there to follow his orders. He didn't believe in love; his marriage had been arranged before he was even born. What Rebecca failed to realize was that hers was too. He had already promised her to Duke Kyle of Ryonshire's son. He was not about to let their good family name get tainted by some ratty little peasant boy. He was a servant boy! Practically a slave. Angered, the baron left the ballroom to get something done that would remind the insignificant little urchin of his place.

That same night the baron called Duke Kyle and his son in for a meeting. He told them that they need not delay any longer, and the wedding would be held the day after tomorrow. This would give the cooks one whole day to prepare, and the seamstress 24 hours to come up with a dress. The duke was delighted and agreed wholeheartedly. His son, however, had been one of the boys that Rebecca had offended last night. Apparently multiple times. He did not want her any more than she wanted him. He grumbled and made his feelings known, but in the end he had no more of a choice then Rebecca had, and reluctantly agreed to go along with the wedding.

The next morning, Jeremiah was informed of the ceremony even before Rebecca knew what was going on. He had been woken early and told that his job for the day was to help with all the decorations. However, before starting he had to go to the throne room and see the baron personally. Perplexed, saddened, and angry, he was already a wreck when he entered the room. He was flanked by two guards who escorted him up to the throne and told him to kneel.

Jeremiah's anger grew. This guy was setting himself up like a king. Sure he was rich and had a fancy title, but he was not a king. Making anyone bow before him as he sat on his high-backed fancy chair was utterly humiliating. However, Jeremiah was only a peasant boy serving the baron to help provide for his family. So whatever the baron told him to do, no matter how degrading, he had to do it.

"Good morning, child." The baron said, wearing a huge fake smile as he looked down his nose at Jeremiah.

Jeremiah did not return the greeting. He stayed still, down on one knee, head bowed as he stared at the polished marble floor. Seething about the unfairness of it all. Calling him a child only fueled his anger.

This did not bother the baron in the least. On the contrary, he seemed to enjoy it. "I have a special task for you today." The baron announced happily, then when he still got no response, his tone suddenly changed. "Look at me when I am speaking to you!" The baron growled, glaring at Jeremiah. Slowly, Jeremiah raised his head and made eye contact with the baron. For a moment the baron was taken aback by the look of pure hatred he saw, but then his surprise faded into a villainous smile. He was getting through to the boy, after all. "You are to go into town and spread the joyful news around that my daughter is *deep in love* with Sir Tomas Edwardias Livingston, son of Duke Kyle Alexander Livingston, both of the noble town of Ryonshire." He paused for effect, watching with glee as Jeremiah's face grew darker. "You will invite everyone you see to the wedding, which will be held tomorrow at noon." With no response from Jeremiah, the baron added, "Have you got all of that?" His voice was thick with malice as he spat the words at him.

"Yes, sir." Jeremiah growled, then, without waiting to be dismissed, turned and ran from the room. He continued to run all the way to Rebecca's room, anger and sadness welling up inside him as tears threatened to fall from his eyes. He threw open the door and entered without even knocking.

The baron's daughter was sitting on her bed reading a book, blissfully unaware of anything going on around her. She jumped when the door opened, and her book fell closed, losing her page. Anger on her face, she was about to yell something, and then she looked up to see who it was. "Oh, it is only you." She smiled. "Do you not know how to knock?"

She teased. Her smile faded when she saw the look of fury on Jeremiah's face.

"Tell me it is not true." He said through gritted teeth, glaring at her, trying unsuccessfully to hold back his emotions. He was furious, brokenhearted, and not thinking clearly.

She couldn't understand why he was so upset. She thought last night had gone wonderfully. She finally saw him, really saw him, for the first time. She realized his kindness, his sweetness, his lovingkindness, and knew that he would never leave her. He wanted to spend time with her and would not run away and leave her heartbroken. She was sure he had felt it too. When he touched her gently on her face, it had sent chills throughout her entire body. Sure, he was tall and scrawny compared to Axel, but his arms felt so very nice when they had been holding her tight. In that moment, when they danced for the first time, she knew that they were going to be together forever. So why was he standing in her doorway looking like he wanted to kill her? "Jere, whatever is the matter? Are you alright?"

"Say it is not true." He repeated, the hatred showing clearly on his face. He banged his fist on the door frame in frustration.

"What in the world is going on? Say what is not true?" She got up and walked closer to where Jeremiah stood. His eyes followed her, but he did not move, nor did his expression change. She tried to caress his cheek with her hand but he grabbed her wrist and held it tight. "Stop! You're hurting me!" She cried, pulling against his iron grip.

"I got orders this morning to start putting up decorations for a wedding." Jeremiah said icily, not letting her go.

Rebecca stopped struggling and asked cautiously, "Who is getting married?"

"You are." He answered, releasing her wrist rather abruptly. He turned away from her with his arms crossed, trying to calm himself down.

Rebecca almost fainted. She couldn't believe it. She knew now why Jeremiah was so upset. She was supposed to be getting married, and he was not to be the groom. She knew this had to be her father's doing, and she did not plan on going through with it. An arranged marriage may be fine for some people, but there was no way she was going to let them destroy the love that she had only just found. They had only been together for one night and already her heart was breaking! How quickly her foolish young heart fell in love! "It most certainly is not true!" Rebecca said stubbornly.

Still not turning to face her, Jeremiah said dejectedly, "I'm supposed to run around town telling people how in love you are."

Jeremiah allowed Rebecca to gently turn him to face her. She looked into his eyes and said, "I am in love. With you."

His anger melted as she held him close, and he kissed the top of her head. "I'm sorry." He said sincerely, mad at himself for losing his temper like that in front of her.

As way of answer, she grabbed Jeremiah's hand and drug him through the castle with her. To every servant she passed, she ordered them to stop whatever it was that they were doing and insisted that there was not going to be a wedding. She marched right into her father's private quarters, telling the guard outside that she would fire him if he did not let her pass. She flung open the doors without knocking, and marched right up to where her startled father was sitting at his desk. Once he saw who it was he resumed looking at whatever papers were on his desk, ignoring the intrusion.

Jeremiah was still angry with the baron and refused to enter into the room any farther than the threshold.

The baron didn't seem to notice them, so Rebecca pounded a fist down on his desk, glaring at him, and demanding his attention.

"Hello, Rebecca." Her father said in a bored tone, not even bothering to look up at her.

"Father, I demand to know why you seem to think I want to marry some boy I have never even met." Rebecca said, getting right to the point.

Again, he did not look at her. "I do not think you want to marry him." He said simply, "I know that you will marry him."

"I most certainly will not!" Rebecca practically shouted. She stamped her foot in anger.

The baron looked up, clearly aggravated at his daughter's defiance. Then he glanced over and saw Jeremiah standing in the doorway. "Do you not have something you are supposed to be doing?"

"Yes, yes he does." Rebecca answered before Jeremiah could say anything. "He is supposed to be getting ready to marry me."

Jeremiah had been fighting the urge to slug that smug little smile off of the arrogant baron's face when he heard Rebecca speak and looked at her in disbelief. Had he heard her right? Did she really just declare her love for him so boldly in front of her father?

The baron laughed. Actually laughed. Jeremiah couldn't remember even seeing the baron crack a smile that wasn't malicious yet alone laughing. He didn't know what to expect. He didn't know whether he should be laughing with him, or crying. Or punching him in the face. He liked that last option best, but he didn't think any of those actions would really help his cause.

"You are a funny girl, my daughter. It is already arranged for you to be wed tomorrow, and Tomas is greatly looking forward to it. You do not want to break the poor boy's heart, now do you? Now, run along and prepare yourself. You must look proper when I give you away." He went back to his paperwork.

Rebecca growled in frustration and turned to leave, dragging Jeremiah behind her. This time she strode to the guest quarters where she knew the duke and his son were staying. She yanked on the door, and found it locked, so she pounded her fists on it until finally someone came to open it.

Looking extremely exasperated with her, Tomas stood in the doorway and asked her what she wanted.

"Are you the duke's son?" Rebecca demanded. She wasn't paying attention to whatever his name was when her father had said it.

"I only tried to introduced myself as such a total of three times last night." Tomas said curtly, obviously not caring for her any more than she did for him. He was a tall gangly man, with pale skin full of brown freckles. His hair was long, and dark red in color. His dark brown eyes looked down his long, pointed nose at her as if she were nothing but an annoying bit of gum that was stuck to his shoe.

"I demand you call of the wedding. I will not marry you. I refuse. I just cannot-"

"Look, miss," he said, interrupting her ranting, "I am not too thrilled about this either. But it is out of my hands. Our fathers have already arranged it. There is nothing you or I can do to change that."

Rebecca isn't the type of girl that takes orders well. She was used to giving them, and having her own way all the time. There was no way she was going down without a fight. "Fine. Let us just see how well this wedding goes without a bride." With that she stomped off and headed back to her room.

She planned to run away, to take Jeremiah with her, and to live happily ever after.

Why do things never turn out the way you plan them?

That night, while trying to escape her terrible fate, she ran into something much worse. She met a monster. A monster that killed her love and almost killed her too.

When Rebecca awoke the next morning, the sunlight hurt her eyes and felt much too hot on her skin. She had a terrible burning thirst in her throat that would not go away. She followed a delicious aroma to a nearby trail where some hunters were out looking for deer.

Soon, the hunters became the hunted, and Rebecca realized a horrifying truth: she had become the monster.

Chapter Two

The farther away they got from the mysterious cave, the louder the world seemed to get. The sky was a beautiful blue above them and they could hear the birds singing merrily in the trees, and the sound of their wings flapping madly as they walked by and they flew away. Each new sound seemed precious to them now, after being in the strange void that surrounded The Wizard's cave. Even the sounds of the tiniest woodland creatures lightened their spirits considerably.

When at long last Axel was back inside his house again, he tried to think of what to bring. How long would he be gone? Should he bring things to create a shelter to spend the night in the woods? He would need food and water, of course, and he didn't leave anywhere without his sword. He had told Conner to bring his bow and arrow, in case they needed to hunt for more food.

"Axel? Where are you going, brother?" Axel's older brother, Jarron, asked as he followed him in from outside. "Our best cow has gone missing, you must stay and help me to search for her. Wes has been searching all day." He stripped off his shirt and threw it over a chair. Then he rested for a moment by leaning against a wall. "Come now, and help us." He said, turning to go back outside.

"I am sorry, Jarron, but I have an important... errand to run. I may be gone for several days." He didn't want to tell him what it was. If The Wizard had wanted him to know, he would have sent for him. Besides, if he failed, and never returned with their father, he would just be giving him a false hope that he was still alive. Or rather, that The Wizard had raised him from the dead. Even inside his head the thought seemed illogical, impossible to conceive as truth. Yet, if there was even the slightest chance that it could happen, he had to try. Whatever the case may be, it was none of his business.

This was Axel's chance to prove that he was worth something. He didn't need anyone else in his life to be complete. He'd show his mother that she was wrong to give up on Father, that there was always still hope. He was going to come back a hero, or not come back at all.

"What is more important than Sadie?" Jarron complained, still going on about the cow.

Axel had five siblings in total: His oldest brother, Jarron, the twins Westley and Sarah that were just two years older than him, his younger sister, Krystal, and their youngest, half-brother, Zacharius. Zacharius was easily the most annoying, although Axel thought Jarron was giving him a run for his money at the moment.

Jarron went on to tell him how he had gone out this morning to feed all the animals (which was usually Axel's job, but he had gotten off the hook because it was his birthday, and then he got the message from The Wizard) and then lastly to milk the cows. This morning, however, their biggest and best cow, Sadie, was nowhere in sight. He complained about how he had gone to get Westley, and together they had searched for her for hours, stopping only temporarily to eat something for lunch. Now, Jarron was coming back to the house to get something for supper. However, one look into the kitchen where their mother and Sarah were busily working away told him that the food was not quite ready yet.

No one wanted to have to deal with their step-father's fury if he found out that the cow was gone. Their step-father always complained that he was too old to go out and work himself, but Axel (and most of everyone else in the village) thought that he was just plain lazy. He would, however, walk around and check to see if everything was going smoothly.

Despite his anger at the missing animal, Jarron's curiosity got the better of him. He had to know what The Wizard wanted from Axel. Jarron was the oldest, if anyone got called to see The Wizard, it should have been him. His jealousy only helped to fuel his anger toward his brother. So when he asked, "What did The Wizard want?" it sounded more like a demand than a simple question to satisfy his curiousness.

"The Wizard gave me a mission and I must leave as soon as possible." Axel said simply, ignoring his brother's evil glares and quickly packing a few more things into his pouch before heading out the door.

Jarron stood there speechless for a minute, then ran to the door yelling angrily for Axel to wait and explain more. He also wanted his help to find Sadie. How could Axel just run off on him like that?

As Axel walked in the direction of Conner's house, he saw that Conner was already waiting, with a similar pouch of his own and his bow and arrows slung across his back.

"What was it your brother was saying, Axel? Something about a cow?" Conner's house was only a few down the road from Axel's, and so he could hear his brother still shouting for him to come back.

"Yea, she may have been stolen, for none of the others are missing." Axel replied.

"I knew a man once who loved cows. He had many, and they all had names, and he raised them as if they were his own flesh and blood. There was this one time when-"

"Conner! Will you calibrate your concentration for a small moment?" said Axel, clearly annoyed that he was still going on about the cow, or cows in general. This was not a time for focusing on one stupid creature that happened to be missing. There was something bigger going on here. Much bigger. "Now, where are we headed?"

"How should I know?" Conner replied simply, shrugging his shoulders.

"You are a navigator, are you not? You should know!" Axel's frustration could be heard in his voice. "Did you not hear a thing The Wizard said?"

Conner smiled sheepishly at his friend and said, "Uh, what are we looking for again?"

Axel sighed. Why had he ever agreed to let Conner come along? "The Wizard said: Go, and look for the bent tree limb. How we are supposed to find *The* bent tree limb in a forest that is full of bent tree limbs, I do not know."

Conner fumbled through his pouch and found his compass. He figured the best place to find a bent tree limb was in the forest, so that was the direction they headed.

They continued to walk until late in the night. Conner's stomach had been growling for hours now, and his feet were killing him. They should have stayed at Axel's house and ate the supper that his mother and sister were preparing. Then they could have gotten a good night's sleep and set out in the morning. Maybe even Axel's brothers would want to come along. Or his sister, Sarah. Conner wouldn't have minded that at all. She was older, though, and thought of Conner more as a little brother than anything else. Still, it would be nice to have some company while walking along. Axel was focused and determined on his goal, and so was not very talkative.

Finally, when the only light left was the little bit from the moon, Axel decided to stop and rest for the night. He gathered up some sticks to make a shelter for them while Conner went out to hunt for their supper. Being extremely hungry, Conner used his bow and arrows to catch them the first thing he saw: squirrels. One for Axel and one for himself. He was rather skilled with his bow (which was a good thing because of how dark it was), and only needed one arrow to take the poor creatures down. After he speared the first one, he retrieved his arrow from deep in its belly and wiped it clean before loosing it again on the second squirrel.

After making a fire and roasting their tiny meals, however, both Conner and Axel were still hungry. So Axel got out some of the bread that he had packed for them in his pouch. Conner had brought some too, but his had all been eaten bit by bit on the walk through the woods. Reluctantly, Axel shared his bread with the still starving Conner.

The next morning, Axel woke up as soon as the sun started to rise and he set to disassemble the shelter he had built, saving his rope and putting it back into his pouch. Conner still lay on the ground, his mouth hanging slightly open in a pile of drool. Axel shuddered as he thought of all the disgusting things that could have entered his mouth as he slept. Instinctively, he stuck his tongue out in a look of disgust. He dressed, and then shook Conner awake. As was his usual morning ritual, Conner immediately started fussing over his hair.

*****

"There they are." A red haired girl whispered to her sister as two men entered into the tavern where they sat waiting. She watched them closely as they pushed the doors open and then looked around uncertainly.

The girl's name was Destiny. She and her sister lived here in Shyloh, only a few blocks away from the bar where they now sat. Normally they would not be found in such a place, but today they had been called by The Wizard and sent on a special mission.

Destiny's bright red hair fell just beyond her shoulders in the back, but was much shorter and slightly choppy in the front. (She insists on cutting it shorter in the front because it always gets in her way. Much to the dismay of her sister who believes that women should not cut their hair like men do) Her green eyes surveyed the men who had just walked in. They both looked like ordinary peasants, just like The Wizard had said they would. Which did make it much more difficult to tell them apart from all the other peasants in the world, but really, what's the worst that could happen?

"How can you know for sure?" Her sister replied.

Destiny smiled her mischievous smile. She didn't really know for certain, but she couldn't just pass up the possibility that it might be. "The Wizard said that one was tall and thin, with dark hair and eyes, and the other was large with bright blue eyes. It must be them!"

They had received a message at their house this morning telling them to go see The Wizard. Immediately they had left, and ventured into the woods to find him. Much to the distress of Destiny's sister, Meriah, who said that two ladies going into the woods by themselves not accompanied by any men was unsafe. Not to mention the fact that they had packed absolutely no provisions and had no idea how far they would be traveling or how long it would take to get there. Destiny had just laughed at her sister and told her that Destiny herself was the scariest thing in the woods, and that she had nothing to worry about.

Where Destiny was slim and hour-glass shaped, her sister still had a bit of baby fat here and there and was shaped more like a pear. Destiny was the type that didn't care what anyone else thought about her, she would dress the way she wanted and speak to whoever she wanted and pretty much just do whatever she wanted whenever she wanted to do it. Meriah, on the other hand, was the sensible one who was always trying to keep her sister in check. She was only a year older than Destiny, but she sometimes acted like she was her mother. This was mostly because they had been separated from their parents when they were both very young, and they had to fend for themselves until they were much older and an elderly lady found them and took them in as her own.

They ventured far into the woods until they were both quite lost. As leaves and twigs crunched beneath their feet, they saw several woodland creatures run away in fear. As the day dragged on, hunger started to settle in and the girls were sorry that they hadn't brought any food along with them. Starting to get tired, they sat down a bit for a rest. After a few minutes, Meriah decided to look around for some wild berries. Before long, she found what she was looking for. It wasn't a lot, but it helped them to get a little strength back before continuing their journey.

An hour or two later they came to a small clearing in the middle of which was a very small cave. As soon as the girls saw it, they felt instantly drawn to it, and were unable to look away. They slowly walked towards it, and without hesitation entered into the unknown.

The ground immediately sloped downward at a very harsh angle. There was a faint light down below that seemed to be bobbing up and down, waiting for them to follow it. Curiously, the girls cautiously started down the steep slope.

When at last the ground began to even out, they were in a large room, with three separate tunnels leading out of it. (Not counting the one they had just come out of.) The strange light was now high above them, and did not offer them any help in deciding which way to go next. Each tunnel had a stripe painted on the wall above it, each in a different color. The one to their right was red, in the middle was blue, and lastly, on the left, was yellow. Which one should they choose? What lay waiting for them in the darkness of each? Searching around the room for any sort of clue, Destiny looked down and noticed they were standing on what appeared to be a giant stone tablet with words carved into it.

There is danger ahead, and even more behind. One way will lead to your freedom, while another will lead to certain death. The last of these, however, is the one that you seek, if magic is what you hold dear. Let the sun shine over your escape if that is what you wish, but I, my friend, have gone inside to hide beside the river.

Both Destiny and her sister were very confused by this text, and had to read it over several times before they could make any sense out of it. Meriah concluded that "the river" probably meant the blue passage, meaning that the one they needed was beside it. Since the blue one was in the middle, this didn't really help much. However, if the "sun shining over their escape" meant the yellow one, then the only possible option left would be the red one. But red was usually a color associated with bad things. Blood was red. Fire was red. If they were wrong, they could die.

Making up her mind, Destiny headed towards the tunnel with the red slash of paint above it. Terrified, her sister grabbed her arm to stop her. "Are you certain that is the right one?"

"There is only one way to find out." Destiny said, grabbing her sister's hand and dragging her along. Destiny stopped right outside the tunnel, and took a deep breath before crossing over into the darkness. She glanced at her sister, so still looked uncertain, and tried to give her a reassuring smile. Then she held her breath and stepped into the tunnel.

Nothing happened.

Destiny let out a sigh of relief, and then smiled widely at her sister. "We did it!" She exclaimed, laughing joyfully at their success.

Suddenly the bobbing light was back, and waiting impatiently at the far end of the tunnel. They followed the light on and on through many more tunnels until they were certain that they would never find their way home again. At long last they came to another large room. This one, however, had no other way out. The strange light floated up to the ceiling and stayed there. The girls looked around in confusion. *What do we do now?* Destiny looked to the floor for another inscription but there was nothing. The room was completely void of anything whatsoever.

"DESTINY AND MERIAH OF SHYLOH. ARE YE READY TO BEGIN YOUR JOURNEY?"

The loud voice startled the girls so much that they both jumped and fell over backwards on top of each other.

Destiny stood up, dusted herself off, and tried to look for the source of the voice. "Uhm... yes?" She said uncertainly.

"YE ARE TO GO TO THE BENT TREE LIMB TO FIND THE MIGHTY DRAGON CALLED AXEL. HE SHALL BE ACCOMPANIED BY A BOY NAMED CONNER."

The Bent Tree Limb? The Wizard was sending them to the tavern back in Shyloh? Why couldn't he have just said so when he summoned them? It would have saved them a lot of trouble.

The Wizard went on to explain what they would look like, but that was all the information he gave them. After the room had gone quiet and their ears had stopped ringing from the deafening voice that was The Wizard, Destiny and Meriah turned back to the tunnel they had come out of earlier to try to find their way back. The tunnel, however, was not there. They were standing at the entrance of the cave, just a few steps from being outside. How they ended up there, they will never know. After pondering this a few moments, the girls headed out and tried to find their way back to their hometown.

So this was where they found themselves now, and this was where they were going to stay until they found who it was that The Wizard wanted them to look for.

The two men walked cautiously into the bar, looking around as if searching for someone, or something. Perhaps they were just lost.

"Look, Meriah, they seek something also. We must approach them, quickly now, follow me." The red-headed sister got up from their table, trying to be discreet and not look as if she was charging at the strangers. The long black dress she wore billowed slightly behind her as she swiftly made her way to the front doors. Reluctantly, her sister followed a little way behind her.

"You two seem to be lost." Destiny said as she reached the newcomers.

The taller man laughed. "You know not the truth in that!" He said, smiling down at her.

The girl wasted no time with small talk, and cut right to the point. "I would not be so certain of that, my friend. How else could I know that The Wizard has sent you here?"

The man's mouth dropped open in shock. It was exactly the reaction Destiny had wanted. "Axel, did you hear what the lady said? She knows The Wizard-"

"We are seeking the bent tree limb, Conner." Axel interrupted him rather loudly, ignoring the two women that stood in his way of getting to the bar. "We have only momentarily stopped here to have a drink, and then we shall continue on our way." Axel said, still talking to Conner. Then he turned to the girls to address them for the first time. "Good day to you, ladies." With that, he rudely pushed past the girls and walked up to the bartender.

Destiny gave Meriah an "I told you so" look.

"You are in the right place then." Meriah called after him. "This is The Bent Tree Limb." She laughed, pointing to a sign that hung above the door that the two had apparently missed.

Just then, a man sitting at the bar with a large glass of beer in his hand turned to look at the strangers. "Yes. The right place indeed." He said, getting up. He was clad all in black, with a long jacket that brushed the floor as he stood. His face was hidden by a large black hood that he kept pulled up over his head. He had a muscular build, although he was tall and slim. All eyes focused on him as he spoke. The end of his long blonde hair could be seen poking out of his hood and resting on his chest. Using both his hands, he slowly lowered his hood, revealing his face to the crowd. He was unbelievably handsome, with dark eyes that seemed to have no color. It seemed only one other person in the tavern knew his face.

"Dante?" Conner asked incredulously, staring wide-eyed at the mysterious man.

"Dante?" Axel repeated, clearly lost in confusion, as he looked the man over and then returned his attention to Conner. "You know this man, Conner?"

The man's face showed no emotion as he stared back at Conner. Did he even recognize him? It was hard to tell.

The two girls stood just behind of Axel and Conner, watching the events unfolding before them intently.

"Dante Sinclaire; An old friend from The Academy." Conner said impatiently, not taking his eyes off the stranger. This moment was important; Conner could feel it. This was Dante Sinclaire. Someone he had not seen since graduation. Someone he was never supposed to see again. If Sinclaire was here, then so was the person that he was meant to watch... If only Axel knew of his true destiny; his *real* identity... If only he knew how dangerous it could be to be running into Dante Sinclaire...

"What are you doing here?" Conner asked, uncharacteristically serious.

"My... duty has brought me here." Dante said, choosing his words carefully. His voice was as deep and mysterious as the rest of him.

They were already attracting the attention of those around them. The bartender glared at them and asked again if they wanted anything to drink. Apparently they hadn't heard him the first time. Or the second time. When again they didn't respond, he told them if they weren't here to buy anything, they didn't need to be here. They continued to ignore him.

"Duty?" asked Axel, "What duty is that?"

"My master sends me." Dante answered casually.

Master. The word rang in Conner's ears. He couldn't mean... Had Dante fallen prisoner to the darkness? Had he been enslaved by the man that he was meant to watch over? He was meant to protect the world from evil, not join it...

"Indeed, and your master would be...?" Conner asked slowly, dreading the answer.

The man just smirked at Conner. After a pause just long enough to make them think he wasn't going to answer, he said, "You will know soon enough."

The man pulled out his sword suddenly and lunged at Conner. He jumped backwards, and dodged the blow just in time, knocking over a table in the process. He didn't have time to get out his bow. By the time he docked an arrow, Dante would strike again. He was fast. Too fast. As he jumped out of the way from another swipe of Dante's deadly blade, he tripped and fell right into the middle of another table.

The sound of glass breaking and splattered ale filled the room along with angry shouts from customers who had just lost their drinks. The bartender started to yell, now furious at their presence. Not only were they going to scare away his customers, but they were destroying his property, too! Just as he was about to leave the bar to interrupt the fight and send them outside, a chair came flying in his direction and smashed against the wall just behind his head. He had dodged it just in time. Surrounded by flying objects, spilled drinks and broken glass, he figured it was best to just hide under his counter and wait it out.

"Conner!" Axel shouted, getting out his own sword, ready to fight in place of his friend. The stranger, however, had no interest in him and continued to try to take his best friend's life. Conner leapt to his feet, doing his best to appear unharmed. Axel couldn't help but notice his now bleeding arm, and could only imagine how much pain his back must be in from landing so harshly on the table. Nevertheless, Conner kept dodging and running, trying to get far enough away to place an arrow into his once best friend. When finally he thought he could accomplish this, he reached back to grab an arrow out of his quiver only to realize that they had all fallen out and were now spread out around the cavern. Conner swore under his breath, then did a barrel roll to his left to avoid another attack.

Axel didn't waste any time and tossed Conner his sword as soon as he had picked himself back up off the ground.

Conner wasn't as skilled with a sword as he was his bow, but he had had a little bit of training back at The Academy. Conner's skills were no match for Dante's, and so he used the sword mostly just to block Dante's blows rather than attack offensively. He tried to look for his lost arrows amidst all the fighting, but found it to be a hopeless cause.

As the fight progressed, the small tavern got more and more destroyed. More people got angry, and before they knew it, everyone was engaged in combat. Those without weapons swung punches at whoever was nearest to them, and the few who did have swords clashed them together in a mass of chaotic anger. Every now and again Conner and Dante would break apart and have to defend themselves against others, but for the most part they just focused on each other.

The girls didn't know what to do, and presently noticed a small child sitting calmly at the bar. She was ignoring everything that was going on around her, except for the central battle between Conner and Dante. Somehow through the chaos she never lost sight of them. Curious, Destiny tried to make her way over to her, mostly to make sure that she was alright, but she was cut off by a rather large man being flung in her direction and her sister pulling her out of the way just in time to avoid being slammed to the ground under the great weight of his limp body.

Moments earlier, Dante had plunged his blade into the poor drunken man's stomach. He did not even pause to acknowledge the life that had been lost, but continued with even more power against Conner, as if the evil act fueled his body and strengthened him.

Destiny noticed the fallen man, and made her way over to help him where he had landed just a few feet away from her. With the constant moving battle raging all around, getting to him was actually harder than one would think. He was weak when she reached him, and he looked scared to death of her, but Meriah helped calm him down. The fact that he was still conscious was good. He was still alive. A few minutes more and she wouldn't have been able to save him. "This will only take but a moment, I give you my word." Destiny said to him. Then she proceeded to push up her sleeves and wave her hands above his wounds. She closed her eyes, and her body swayed a bit in a chanting motion, and in only a few minutes she was done. Where there was once a bloody gash in the man's middle, was now fresh new skin. Not even a scar remained of his past injury. She helped the man to his feet, and he stared down in amazement at the spot where his wound used to be. He was still covered in blood, ragged ripped clothes, and had lost his shoes somewhere along the way, but other than that he felt absolutely fine. Better than he had in months, maybe even years. He thanked her excessively, and asked what he could do to repay her. Destiny told him it was nothing, and sent him on his way. Expert pickpocket that he was, however, he slipped a few gold coins into her pouch without her noticing before leaving the pandemonium of the tavern.

At long last Axel found a discarded sword and decided to use it to try to help Conner defeat Dante. He worked his way back to them and tried to sneak up behind the stranger, planning to stab him in the back before he even knew he was there. Dante was just too quick. He pulled out another sword and began excellently sparring away with both Axel and Conner. Conner, however, was tiring, and Axel could tell. He'd already been scratched twice, not including the cut on his arm from when he first smashed into the table. One little mistake and he would lose his best friend. As it was, Conner was already losing a lot of blood. Too much blood.

All of a sudden there was a rather large man in the middle of everything. He appeared right in front of Axel, blocking him and Conner from Dante. He wore grand robes of the darkest black, and an exquisite golden crown upon his head, hiding most of his brown wavy hair. He appeared to be some sort of dark king. As soon as he appeared, Dante replaced both his swords in their scabbards, and knelt down on one knee. "Master." he said, bowing his head to the newcomer.

The small girl who had been watching everything Dante did from the bar stood behind him, and gasped when she saw the great king. Dante cleared his throat and she gasped again, remembering that she was supposed to be copying him. She took a few steps forward and knelt down next to Dante, bowing her head to the king, just like he had.

The strange king glared around at everyone with his piercing blue eyes, threw out his hands, and yelled, "ENOUGH!"

That was all anyone could remember before they were all knocked into unconsciousness.

Chapter Three

The scared bartender was still hiding under his counter. He had heard the crashing chaos going on around him, and then heard a shout louder than anything else. Then rather abruptly he heard... nothing. Complete and utter silence. He waited a bit, expecting the fight to begin again at any moment. When no sounds came, he slowly lifted his head to peer out at his destroyed establishment. What he saw shocked him. Yes, his place was a wreck, most likely beyond repair, but there was absolutely no trace of anyone left that had caused it. He was completely alone in the tavern. It was as if a tornado had come in, destroyed everything he owned, and left out the front door. It was rather amazing that he still had four walls and a roof after all that had gone on in here. Even as he was thinking it, one of the small swinging entrance doors fell off its hinges and crashed to the ground. The sudden noise made him jump, and it took him several minutes to realize that he wasn't dreaming. His life's work had been destroyed and he was left with nothing. How would he ever pay to feed his family? Sure he had a little money now, but as soon as it was gone that was it. He had no other source of income. His wife had a baby on the way and they already had one little girl at home. How was he supposed to explain all this? He had no proof of anything, and no witnesses save himself. For all anyone else knew he could have gone mad and trashed the place himself. Even his most faithful customers had deserted him. He spotted one lone cup in the back of the room that had somehow avoided getting broken, and he walked carefully to it, sidestepping debris across the way. He picked it up gingerly, as if it was a precious child, and carried it back to his counter. He still had a few bottles of wine left, and he sat on his stool and uncorked one. He was about to pour it into the glass, but then stopped. He looked around at his isolation. No one else would want any because there was no one else here. He put the bottle to his lips and before long it was empty. He drank himself to sleep, his head resting on the counter, and he did not wake until the next day.

When he awoke the next day, he stumbled out of the tavern, still half asleep, wondering why it was so quiet out. As he continued to look around, the deserted town helped to bring him back to reality. He no longer seemed to be in a stupor, rather on the contrary, he was alert and starting to panic.

"Where is everyone? Stephen! Makaylah! Is anyone out there?" He walked around curiously, shouting out the names of all the missing merchants. When no one responded, he began to run around to all the nearby houses, calling out names and slamming his fists on doors.

Suddenly he stopped, dead in his tracks. He turned around slowly, now facing the opposite direction of the tavern. He started to run, increasing his speed all the way down to the other end of the road. He turned down several streets until anyone else who did not know the way would be completely lost. Finally the man found the house he was looking for. He didn't bother to knock. He barged right in and started screaming for someone named Seriah.

He stood in the doorway to their bedroom, sweating and out of breath from running the whole way here. He didn't know what to do. After a while he just fell to his knees and began to weep.

*****

Destiny was the first one to wake up. She groggily lifted her head from the hard ground. She looked around in confusion. They were no longer in the tavern. Instead, they were in the woods, at the bottom of a great dirt pit. Only a few of them were here; Her and her sister, and the two men that had entered the bar. The man who had started the fight with Conner was nowhere in sight. Nor were any of the other people who had been in the tavern with them.

Conner was the next to wake up. As soon as he was fully awake, his hands flew to his head. "How is my hair?"

Destiny laughed as he frantically tried to fix it. Every time he found a new leaf or tiny little twig in it he would freak out.

"What just happened?" asked Meriah as she got up. "Where are we?" She patted down her crinkled navy blue dress. It was much like her sister's black one; long with wide bell sleeves; except that Meriah's was much more modest in the front.

They look down at Axel, who is the last to awaken. Destiny knelt down next to him, but instead of shaking him gently, she yelled in this face, "Wake up!"

He is awake instantly, and looks up into her eyes for the first time. He is taken in by her sweet beauty, and smiles as he loses himself in the moment.

"Axel? Are you not well?" she asked, poking a finger at his chest. It was enough to break his trance, and he shook his head to clear it. He sat up and looked around at the giant dirt crater they were in. The woods seemed to be high above them, but were they even the same woods that they had come through earlier?

"Yes, yes, I am fine." He said, standing up and pushing her aside to look around. "What is this place?"

"You know only as much as the rest of us." Destiny said stubbornly, annoyed by his behavior.

Just then a sudden realization dawned on Axel. How had the girls in the tavern known their names? Neither he nor Conner had introduced themselves, and yet they seemed to know both of their names already. Not to mention the fact that they had known that they had been to see The Wizard. He pondered this for a moment. Perhaps they had been following them? But then how would they have gotten to the Bent Tree Limb before them? Could they really trust these girls? They didn't even know their names...

After Conner had stopped freaking out about his hair, he started freaking out about the place where they now found themselves. "So, we could stay in this bleak place and talk, or we can find a way out of here!" He cried, the panic welling up inside of him. Had he not known that seeing Dante was a bad sign? See, he was right! What on earth had the king done to them? Where had he thrown them? How had he done it so easily? And to only the four of them? Without even laying a hand on them? And why? Why??

"What happened to Sinclaire and the rest of the men in the tavern?" Axel asked, thinking it best not to worry Conner any more than he already was. He'd confront the girls later.

"I do not know, and I care not for them at the moment!" Conner was starting to sound frantic, and he stood there nervously twisting a lock of his hair.

Meriah ignored them and started to run towards a dirt wall. Both of the boys stared at her, and Conner shouted something in terror, but neither of the girls were worried. As Meriah ran, she began to change. Her dress fell away as she shrunk and grew feathers. After only a moment, she was flying instead of running. She had transformed herself into a beautiful hyacinth macaw, and was now soaring high above them in the sky. The feeling was exhilarating; wonderful; peaceful. The feeling of being free.

Conner screamed, and jumped up into Axel's arms, who promptly dropped him to the ground.

"It is less steep here!" She called down to them, from the opposite end of the ravine. "Come, and climb up on this side." Her voice sounded different, much more bird-like than her normal human voice. Nonetheless, the rest of the group could still understand her quite well.

"A brilliant idea indeed." said Conner, somewhat sarcastically. He was the first to follow Meriah to the other side of the pit. Axel followed, and Destiny was behind him. Quite suddenly, Conner turned around and darted back to the spot where he had woken up. He circled around, staring at the ground. Then he started to look under every rock he saw, and every stick.

"Have you gone mad? What are you doing?" Axel asked, grabbing Conner's arm to stop him.

"Where is my bow? My arrows?" Conner yelled, not bothering to even look up at Axel as he spoke. He wrenched himself free of Axel's grasp and continued his search.

Then realization stuck Axel like a blow to the chest as he looked around and noticed that his sword was missing too. He swore. "She was my father's sword! A family heirloom!" Now he was upset too. That sword had been very special to him. His father had passed it down to him just before he died. He had never actually seen his father use it, but he had told him that it had been in Axel's family for as long as anyone could remember. Axel remembered the last words his father had said to him after telling him the glory of the sword: "She belongs to you, son. Use her to protect others, and yourself. Indeed, 'twas your father's..." Axel didn't know why he had called himself "father" instead of just saying it was his, but he figured that he wasn't quite all there since he was slowly dying. He didn't even really know why his father died. He had been very sick for a long time. They had taken him to several doctors, and sent for experts that lived far away to come and see him. His sickness simply baffled everyone, and even the best medicines could not help to ease his symptoms, let alone his rapidly declining health. He got progressively worse as the days went on, and when he died, Axel's mother had told him that he should rejoice that his suffering was finally over. His mother always did see the bright side of things. A true optimist.

The short girl just smiled at him. "Who needs weapons when you have magic?" she said, effortlessly producing a magic orb in the palm of her hand.

"You!" Axel's loss suddenly turned to rage and it was directed at Destiny. "What have you done with our swords? I knew that you were untrustworthy! How is it that you knew our names? Or about The Wizard? And now you have taken our only means of defense from us! What evil have you brought upon us?"

Destiny was taken aback. "Evil?" She asked, outraged, not knowing what else to say. Words failed her as the frustration of his words bubbled up inside of her. Evil? How dare he say that about her and her sister! Evil! Really?! What evil had she ever done to him? How dare he even think for a moment that she would take his stupid sword! What could she possibly want with a sword?

"Look, *sir*," Destiny said icily, spitting the words out slowly, "I know your name only because The Wizard spoke it to me! I was sent here to help you! If you do not want my help, I will gladly leave you to find your own way!"

Axel glared at her, but did not respond. Destiny crossed her arms and turned away from him.

"Destiny." Meriah said, in the tone of a mother reprimanding her child. Destiny acted as if she could not hear her sister. Meriah turned to look at Axel, who was now ignoring them and looking for his sword. "We must not turn one against another." She said in her calming voice. "The Wizard said that all of us were needed to succeed."

Axel looked up and glared at them both in turn. He didn't know what to believe. Would The Wizard really send for women? Call them to help men? Of course not! How illogical it all sounded! If anything it was Conner and Axel that were called to help them, not the other way around. Axel was fuming. He had a million things he wanted to ask, but finally just settled on, "Who are you anyway, that The Wizard should call upon you to help us?"

"I am Destiny Starr, of Shyloh, and this is my sister, Meriah Grace." Destiny answered, the words coming out sharper than she'd intended as she tried to calm herself down. "The Wizard sent a messenger to our humble home saying to leave immediately. When we found The Wizard, he said to us, 'Go unto the Bent Tree Limb and wait for the one that is called Axel Rynne of Salbris, and the one who is with him called Conner.' Now, are you not Axel? And is he not Conner? You must trust me, for The Wizard said that you would come and it was so." Destiny was frustrated. Her stubborn side was showing, and she was speaking up for herself; a trait that was frowned upon in her society. Women were to be "seen and not heard". Well, not this woman.

"If that be so," Axel said, testing her, "Then why did The Wizard not tell us?"

"I do not know the ways of The Wizard." Destiny retorted. "Only what he told me."

There was a moment's pause in which Axel and Destiny just stared at each other, before Axel finally broke the silence. "Nevertheless, I do not have any magic. I need my sword to fight!"

Destiny just rolled her eyes and crossed her arms. *Men.* She sighed.

At this point, Meriah could tell they weren't getting anywhere. Destiny was stubborn, and always thought she was right, even when she knew she wasn't. So Meriah swooped down and transformed right next to Conner.

Conner jumped, and screamed out a little, at the sudden sight of a girl next to him. Especially a naked one. Meriah wasn't used to transforming in front of anyone but her sister, and didn't realize until it was too late that she had forgotten her dress. It was very difficult to transform back into clothing, and with no one around but another girl, it usually wasn't too big of an issue to be undressed for a minute or two before she could get her clothes back on. Horribly embarrassed, Meriah blushed redder than Destiny's hair as she ran to cover herself. She pulled her dress down over her head quickly and walked slowly back over to Conner. She apologized for her indecency, repeatedly, then, trying to change the subject back again, said, "What about you, Conner? Do you know any magic?"

"Only a little." He confessed, blushing ever so slightly. He chuckled nervously, then added, "Just the basics from the Academy."

Destiny rolled her eyes again. "Come, Meriah, they are hopeless." She laughed a bit before turning to walk up the hill. Her sister smiled and transformed back into a bird. She soared ahead effortlessly. "Meriah! Come, back here and walk like the rest of us!" Destiny called up to her, picking up her discarded dress and waving it in the air at her sister.

The bird laughed. It was a rather strange sound, something like a cross between a parrot and a crow's call. "You are just jealous of my wings!" She soared higher, circling around her in the air, purposely showing off.

Almost to the top of the hill, the girls look back and realize that the guys have barely moved. "Are you coming, you slowest of men? Or must we come back for you?" Destiny called down to them.

Reluctant to leave without his sword, Axel slowly turned around to face the girls, and, realizing how far ahead they were, broke into a run to catch up to them. Caught off guard by his friend's sudden burst of speed, Conner is left behind and has to scramble to keep up with him.

Almost to the top of the hill, the guys look back and realize that the guys have barely moved. "Hey you comin' you showed of men? You must be no goduck for you?" Dimitry called down to them.

Receiving no answer, almost level slowly turned around to face the group, and became furious when they were broke into a few men that he knew. Chief of which by his friend's sudden scream of power. Conner just yelled and had to stand him to keep up to them.

Chapter Four

When Axel did not return from his "special mission" for several weeks, his family started to get concerned. His mother was frantic, fearing the worst, and his step-father would go out searching with Jarron every day.

After several months had passed, everyone had started to give up hope. Everyone except Jarron. He felt terrible for the way he'd talked to Axel the last time he'd seen him, and he didn't want his last memories of him to be him yelling at him.

There's only one way to find out what happened, Jarron thought as he packed some provisions into a pouch and got ready to leave the house. *I have to go find The Wizard and talk to him myself.*

He spent days walking through the woods, with no sign of anything that might help him find The Wizard. After a week had passed, he was out of provisions, and desperate for something to drink. Just when he thought he couldn't make it any farther, he came to a small town.

The town, however was deserted. There were long abandoned merchant stands set up that were now disintegrating into nothing. "Hello?" He called out to the emptiness. "Is anyone here?" He slowly walked down the dusty street, looking around the houses for any sign of life.

The broken door of the tavern caught his eye and he stepped inside. At first he thought the place was just as barren as the rest of the town, and was about to leave when he noticed an arm on the ground, poking out from behind the bar. Fearing the worst, he took a deep breath and walked slowly forward. Luckily the arm was still attached to a body, but its owner did not look like he was in very good health.

Jarron crouched down next to the man and was relieved to see that he was still breathing. He tried shaking him awake, but it didn't help. Desperate to find out what happened in this town, Jarron looked around for something to help him. He saw one last remaining cup, picked it up and took it outside to where the horse's trough stood. He filled the cup with water, walked back inside, and splashed the contents of the cup in the bartender's face. He awoke with a start.

"Sorry for the rude awakening. Are you ok?" Jarron asked after setting the cup back down on the counter.

"Fine, just... fine." His eyes got real wide as he looked at Jarron. "Who are you? How did you get here? Are there others?" He started poking him to make sure he was real.

"Afraid not." Jarron answered, helping the man to his feet. "Just me. What happened here?"

He explained all about the fight and how the whole town disappeared. "I've been alone ever since."

If Jarron hadn't just seen the barren town and destroyed tavern, he'd think the poor guy had just imagined the whole thing. He tried his best to describe Axel and his idiot friend whose name he couldn't remember, asking if he could remember seeing them at the fight.

"It's been so long, I normally wouldn't remember, however, the large fellow was the one who started all the fighting." He said accusingly.

"I am sorry; I am sure he had good reason."

"Good reason?! They destroyed my livelihood!"

"I really am sorry, sir."

The man waved a hand dismissively at him and asked if there was anything else he wanted. Jarron told him he was out of provisions and he really could use a place to stay for the night.

"Pick a house, any house. None of them are occupied anymore." he said as he went to fetch him some food and something to drink.

*****

Destiny led the way out of the pit, with her sister following closely behind her. Looking around, she realized that they were deep in the heart of the forest with absolutely no clue as to which direction they needed to go. She paused at the edge, waiting for the others to catch up.

Conner scrambled out of the pit a few moments later, with Axel lagging the farthest behind, still looking around for any sign of his precious weapon. Upon discovering the fact that they were no closer to knowing where they were now that they were out of the pit, Axel instinctively reached for the pouch that usually hung on his belt that contained his trusty compass. Unfortunately, the pouch and all of its contents were in the same predicament as they were: hopelessly lost. Axel grumbled, his already bad mood growing worse by the minute. He looked around again, but everything looked the same in every direction, unless of course they wanted to retrace their steps back into the hole where they had woken up. Axel wasn't about to admit he was lost, so he pushed ahead and took the lead in a random direction. Much to the protests of Destiny, who found him to be incredibly rude and arrogant and demanded to know how he knew they were going in the right direction. Axel didn't say a word, he just pressed on, leading them deeper and deeper into the woods. They continued on like this for hours, with no sign of civilization. As the day dragged on, their pace became slower as they forced themselves to keep moving.

Axel tried his best to not show any signs of tiring, but Conner had been complaining since they left that he was slowly starving to death. Without his bow and arrows, he had no way to hunt for food, and neither of the boys had any idea what plants were and weren't safe out here in the wild. If only Axel wasn't such a pompous, egotistical, and sexist man and he actually had half a brain to ask the two ladies that were with them. If he'd only stop and let them rest long enough to examine some of the wonders around them. Destiny and Meriah were both very skilled in herbology and could have helped to fill their bellies, and in less than an hour they would have been back on their way. But, alas, Axel trudged on, apparently not caring for anyone but his own self. Finally, long after the sun had already left them, it became too dark to see where they were going. At last, when they came to a small clearing where some of the moonlight shone through to light their path, Axel gave in to his fatigue and collapsed on the ground to rest for the night. Tired, hungry, and still lost, the rest of the group had no objections.

Destiny, making it clear to Axel that she thought their rest was long overdue, gathered up some twigs and started to make a fire. Slowly but surely the small fire licked its way across the wood as it grew larger and brightened up the small clearing.

Meriah busied herself with collecting some berries and herbs, and was trying to clean them off the best she could when she heard a rustling in the woods behind her. She stopped what she was doing immediately, and slowly turned her head towards the noise. It was hard to see anything past the dense tree line, and she dismissed the sound as nothing and went back to her work.

Conner heard it too. "What was that?!" He exclaimed, springing to life in an instant panic. He nervously twisted a piece of his hair in one hand.

Meriah looked up at him with a gentle expression, trying to keep him calm. "Nothing to worry about, I am sure."

Axel rolled his eyes, and laid back down on the ground where he was trying to take a nap. Not that he could really sleep with his stomach constantly reminding him that he hadn't ate anything all day. Not to mention the aching thirst that was taking hold of most of his thoughts. He was dehydrated, as he well knew he had been for most of the day. How was he to accomplish anything if they all died out here in the middle of nowhere? Perhaps The Wizard wanted to reunite him with his father by killing him too. But why make him suffer? Why allow him to drag his best friend down with him? And what was the deal with sending these two girls along? What purpose did they serve? Just then the sound of twigs breaking and leaves being trampled under heavy feet roused him from his suspicions and peaked his interest slightly. He sat up slowly, still not wanting to give up trying to sleep, and looked around curiously for the source of the sound. Conner was on his feet, nervously twitching this way and that at the slightest sound. Meriah was standing next to him, trying in vain to pacify him. Destiny had taken over her job of trying to clean off the food that they had foraged, and had ripped off a small piece of her dress to lay the meal on.

As the sound grew louder, Axel stood and watched closely in the direction of the noise. There was a moments silence, as everyone held their breath in anticipation of the confrontation of whatever it was that was out there. In the sudden silence, Axel wondered if the creature had turned around and decided not to bother them after all. He had just started to sit back down when all of a sudden a great black bear lunged out of the darkness and into the clearing, heading straight for Conner.

Conner screamed louder than anyone had ever heard, and instantly collapsed into a dead faint. Luckily, Meriah was quick enough to push him out of the way so that the beast didn't land on top of him. She lost her footing in the process and tumbled down into the dirt next to Conner.

Axel looked around for something to defend himself and the rest of them, but all he could find was a bunch of broken tree branches and a few very small rocks. If only he still had his sword! That barbaric brute wouldn't stand a chance!

Destiny stood up and gently laid the food down on her small piece of material to keep it clean. She straightened her back, staring at the beast square in the face. She showed no fear, she did not scream out or cower in terror. "Get behind me." she said to no one in particular. Meriah took her advice and dragged Conner as far behind her as they could get without leaving the clearing. Axel, however, protested loudly, clearly thinking that she had lost her mind. Destiny adverted her eyes for only a moment to glare at Axel, and repeated her demand once more. When Axel still refused to listen, Destiny just sighed and focused once more on the black bear. It was easily five times bigger than she was, but instead of running away, she started to run directly at it. Now thoroughly convinced that she was completely insane, Axel ran after her to stop her. He threw a small tree branch at the bear to advert its attention, which bewildered it only momentarily and only helped to increase its anger and focus it on Axel.

Destiny ignored Axel and his many protests at her facing the beast alone. She had already started to change. She was growing larger, and before Axel even knew what was happening she was running on four legs. Her dress ripped and fell off of her, and Axel stopped, staring incredulously at her. He didn't believe what he was seeing. The thing that collided with the bear was not a girl. Not a human one, at least. No, the creature that dug it's claws deep into the bear's hide was a magnificent white tiger. Without so much as a warning growl, the tiger attacked. The bear let out a scream of pain and swiped the tiger off with one of his giant paws. Enraged, the beast stood up on its hind legs growling and swiping its paws out in the direction of the tiger. The tiger was not intimidated. She was quick and lunged at him again, this time bringing her sharp teeth down into the poor bear's neck. Weakened only slightly by the loss of blood, the bear still had enough energy to try to kill his attacker. His paw swiped the tiger once more, this time slicing open her side. Destiny let out a ferocious growl, and you could tell it was personal now. Her next attack would not leave the bear alive.

Axel was defenseless without his sword and it was all he could do to watch and wait as the two beasts fought to the death in front of him. He stood over by Meriah and Conner and waited for the cruel deed to be done. Meriah was kneeling on the ground by Conner, trying to revive him.

Destiny swiftly sliced open the bear's belly with one of her massive paws. It wasn't long after that that she had the bear pinned down and it had breathed its final breath. Exhausted from the fight, Destiny walked away from the bear and laid down on the ground. Meriah came running to her side, grabbing the remains of her dress to cover up her sister as she transformed back. The wound in her side looked much worse on a short little red-headed girl than it did on a great white tiger. Her sister gasped at the blood, and tried to clean it as best she could. Axel turned away respectfully, as to not embarrass Destiny too much. Destiny didn't speak, she just laid on the ground, her eyes shut tight, moaning in agony whenever her sister tried to touch her injury.

"Destiny, you know I am no good at healing, you have got to stop squirming and let me look at it." Meriah reprimanded.

Destiny opened her eyes and lifted her head off the ground slowly to glance down at her side. She was losing a lot of blood, and her head was starting to feel funny as if she might pass out. She laid back down, balled up her fists and waited for the worst. "Go ahead." She said through clenched teeth.

Meriah set to work waving her arms around above the wound. Her eyes were closed, and her body was swaying slightly with the movement. Destiny squirmed and wiggled like a worm caught on a hook, but she stayed strong and did not interrupt her sister. She could feel her strength coming slowly back into her. The place where she had been struck felt as if someone had set it on fire, but Destiny knew it would all be over soon. When she had regained enough strength, she stopped her sister and finished the rest of the work herself. Destiny was an expert at healing, and when she was done there was only the dried blood left over to hint that there was ever any cut there at all.

"Are you... uhm, is everything alright?" Axel asked when she appeared to be finished.

"Never better." Destiny said simply. She started to sit up and her shapeless dress started to fall right off of her. Blushing, Destiny gathered up the material and wrapped it around herself like a towel. Trying to hide his grin, Axel took off his belt and offered it to her to help keep her dress in place. Reluctantly, she accepted his offer. "New plan." She said, after she'd finished fixing up her dress, "We are having bear for supper." She grinned and walked over to the carcass, changing her right hand into a strange half-way transformed paw so that she could use her claw as a knife to cut the meat.

Conner moaned and came to slowly, and Meriah walked over and helped him to his feet. He immediately started to mess with his hair, and it took him a good five minutes to even notice the wild scene that was now before him. Destiny was slicing pieces of meat from a dead bear and putting them on sticks which she handed to Axel to cook over the fire. It took him a while to realize that Destiny wasn't using any tools either. Just her hands, but they didn't really look like hands anymore, they were more paw-like, and she was using one razor-sharp claw to slice into the meat. Conner didn't know what to make of all this. He saw her ripped up dress and tried to formulate in his mind what could have happened. He couldn't, as much as he tried, figure anything out.

Meriah giggled at his obvious bewilderment.

When everyone had eaten their fill, Destiny skinned the rest of the fur off of the bear to use for clothing or shelter. She wanted to make as much use of it as possible. She really hated having to kill the poor animal, but it would have killed them all if she hadn't intervened. The rest of the night passed rather uneventfully, and they resumed their journey in the morning.

When Axel, Conner, Destiny, and Meriah finally found the end of the woods, they found themselves in a very strange place. Apparently they had walked very, very far away from their homelands. How could this place be so very different from their own? It was almost as if they were in a completely other world entirely. They had come from a land where it was customary to have to chop and gather wood, plough in the fields, and harvest and collect corn on a daily basis. This was not the world they found themselves in now. It was Axel's job to milk all of the cows, and take care of all the animals, but where were all the animals in this place? Where were their barns? Their fences? Where did they keep their livestock? The cows and chickens? Were there no animals in this land? They could see no sign of life here. The ground under their feet was hard as a rock, but smooth and stretched out on both sides as far as they could see.

They had walked away from the edge of the woods to find a paved road and many houses. The houses were strange to them, and bigger than any wood houses they had ever seen. Where they even made of wood? It was hard to tell. Most of them were white, and there seemed to be no cracks in them at all! They weren't exactly castles, for they had no towers, but some of them looked like they were stacked on top of each other! It was illogical. How could the smoke from your fire get out if you had no hole in your roof? Then they saw the most bizarre thing of all...

"What kind of strange steed is that?" Conner exclaimed. He was pointing at a round object shooting past them on the road, his face full of admiration and amazement. The thing was black and shiny, but it did not have legs like any animal should. Instead it had wheels. Four of them. And they were fast. Incredibly fast.

"No, they are not horses." Said Destiny, staring as another one drove by. "They seem more like carts, except they drive themselves."

"Look again, sister. There are people in them." Meriah responded, noticing a lady drive by with her arm sticking out of the side window.

"But how is it possible that they come to move the carts without the horses to pull them? Do they use their magic to move the carriages?" Destiny asked. Apparently, it was a busy time of day because suddenly there were a lot of these strange new things going by on the road. "Where are they all going, I wonder?"

"Of more importance, where are we now?" Axel cut in, rolling his eyes in annoyance.

They started to walk down side of the road, seeing more of these new carts in all different shapes and sizes. Suddenly Destiny had a thought. She had no idea if it was even possible, but it would help to explain some of the strange things they were seeing. She turned to Axel and said, "I think a better question may be, when are we now?"

Axel turned away from Destiny, and a few moments later he spotted a young man walking towards them on the sidewalk. He had blonde hair, which was slightly wavy and medium in length. His eyes shone a brilliant blue, with a hint of mischievousness in them. He wore a plain black t-shirt that said "RENT" across the front of it. His pants were of a strange blue material that Axel had never seen before.

Axel glanced around at his friends. Meriah, in her modest long bell-sleeved dress, all covered up, not showing a thing; Destiny in her tighter dress, made from a single large piece of her original dress and tied up with a rope; and Conner, dressed in his usual plain tunic and trousers. Was this the way the people dressed here? How strange he and his friends must look! He wondered for a moment how the women dressed, and the thought passed his mind how funny they would look in this new short sleeved shirts and pants look.

"Pardon me, good sir," Axel said, getting the young man's attention, "Would you be so kind as to tell me the year?"

The man started to laugh. "Did you have too much to drink at your con?" He obviously thought this was all some funny joke, so Axel forced a laugh and nodded.

Axel tried not to panic when he heard the answer.

"Welcome to the future, buddy." The boy continued to laugh as he pushed past them and kept on walking down the street, not realizing how right he really was.

"What is a con?" Conner asked.

Axel rolled his eyes. That was not important now. It appears that they missed out on a lot of time. Over 900 years of it. Somehow, when that dark king crashed into the bar and forced everyone into unconsciousness he had also thrown them into the future. How were they ever going to get back to their own time? They knew nothing of time travel. If you had asked any one of them that same morning, they would have told you it was impossible. Yet here they were, clearly out of place in this extraordinary new world.

Everything happens for a reason, at least that's what Axel's mother always told him. So, the important thing to do now was to find out why they were here, and what they had been sent here to do. They must have some kind of mission here... but how were they supposed to get anywhere or do anything if they knew nothing of this place? They needed to find a place - or perhaps a person - that would tell them everything that they'd missed. They needed to learn how to blend in. If that king was still out there looking for them, they would stick out like a dirty harlot in the middle of a holy church.

Before they had a chance to figure out what they were going to do, they were interrupted by the sound of a man's voice. "What have we here?" It was Dante again, appearing out of thin air right next to Conner. The girl was with him too. She hid behind him, waiting silently for instruction. She was young, with brown hair that fell just to the tips of her shoulders. She had a sweet, round face, and kind, light brown eyes. She had on the same dress from when they'd seen her last; a very simple red one. "Good morning, sleepyheads." Dante said with a smirk. Dante was also dressed in the same long black jacket and trousers, but his shirt was missing, exposing his deliciously toned abs and delightfully hairless chest. The girls had to admit he was attractive. Extremely attractive. It was really hard to focus on his face when his stimulating muscles were showing.

"You!" Axel turned on him, recognizing him as the man from the bar who had started the whole fight. "Have you any good reason at all why I should not smite you here and now?"

Dante pretended to ponder this for a moment and then smiled maliciously. "Alas, I do not." He chuckled evilly.

His long coat billowed slightly in the breeze behind him. It took all of Destiny's concentration to focus on his words and nothing else. She had to remind herself, repeatedly, that he was evil. "And you have no weapons. As it were, as much as it would please me to slay you, I cannot. The Master wishes to take care of you personally. My fight is with Conner."

While Axel wanted to ask a thousand questions, like how he knew about their weapons, or who his master was, Conner didn't give him a chance. He stepped up to Dante, fists balled up tight, ready to fight with his bare hands. "Very well then, let us fight!" It was strange to see Conner acting this way, walking bravely into a fight, instead of running away like a dog with its tail between its legs.

Dante smiled darkly at him. "I was hoping you would say that." He laughed as his fingernails began to grow and automatically sharpen to a point, so that he had five mini-blades on each hand. "Give it your best." Dante said simply, not intimidated in the least by Conner.

Conner swung his fists wildly at Dante, most obviously not used to hand-to-hand combat. Almost immediately he had four tiny slashes through his right arm. He yelled out in pain, but he wasn't distracted for long. Conner flung his leg up and kicked Dante in the stomach. Dante was only winded for a second. He disappeared, and then popped up behind Conner and kicked the backs of his knees. Conner fell to the ground with a loud thud. Now, not only was his arm bleeding, but his hands were too, and most likely his knees were a torn up mess. His pants certainly were.

Axel wanted to step in and help his friend from the start, but Destiny held him back. "You saw what happened the last time. I think it best that you let them settle this themselves." Reluctantly, Axel stepped away from the fight, but not before promising his friend to protect him if things got out of hand.

Conner really didn't want to hurt Dante, but he needed to defend himself. He looked around desperately for something to use as a weapon. There was nothing. They were surrounded by nothing but a bunch of twigs and dead leaves. With the busy road on one side of them, and the wild forest on the other, there weren't very many options for him to choose from. As soon as he had dragged himself to his feet, Dante kicked his side and he fell back to the ground. Dante yelled at him to get up. Weakly, his side aching, his knees and hands bleeding, he got to his feet and put up his fists.

Axel had had enough. "Watch the girl." He said, turning to face the girls, "It is time to finish this." It was obvious that Conner had no chance in this fight, and he wasn't about to just stand by and watch his friend die. He turned and charged at Dante. Caught by surprise, Dante flew sideways and dropped to the ground with Axel on top of him. Next thing Axel knew, however, Dante was gone and he was grasping at the air. By the time Axel was back on his feet, Dante had already resumed his fight with Conner.

Meriah glanced at the girl she was told to watch. She didn't look very threatening. "She is just a cute little-"

"DO NOT CALL ME CUTE!" The girl yelled, suddenly turning to face Meriah and her sister with fierce eyes. She held out her arms and flames began to grow from the palms of her hands. She slowly advanced toward the girls, the flames growing bigger as she got closer. Just then Conner looked over, saw the girl, screamed, and fainted. Axel, ignoring the girl, took the opportunity to punch Dante in the stomach. He disappeared again, and Axel was left slugging the air. This only helped to fuel Axel's anger.

"Katara!" yelled Dante suddenly, re-appearing closer to the torch girl and receding his claws. The girl turned to look at him, lowering the arm that was just getting ready to throw a giant fireball at the girls. "Let us go." Dante's eyes had grown wide with an expression almost like fear on his face. He motioned for the girl to come to him. She nodded, her fire disappeared, and she ran to him. She reached out to touch him and then they were gone.

As suddenly as it all began, it was over. It was so strange; it took them all awhile to believe that it was really done.

"Why... why did they leave?" Asked Meriah, breaking the silence.

"Does it matter? She was about to incinerate us!" replied Destiny. Then she walked over to where the beaten up Conner lay unconscious on the ground. She kneeled down next to him and gently poked his stomach.

Conner awoke with a start. He sat bolt upright and started to immediately mess with his hair. "Wha-? How is my hair?"

"Oh, silence your vain babblings about your hair!" said Destiny, "There are far more important matters at hand." She sighed. "Hold still while I fix up your wounds."

When at last he was done with his hair, he held out his hands for her to look at. They were scraped up from the cement. Easy fix. Only seconds worth of her time. Next she took a look at his knees. The cuts were a little deeper, much dirtier, but basically the same. With a few waves of her hands, the skin renewed itself and his pain was gone. The holes in his pants would remain, and the dirt and dried blood, but any cuts or scratches would cease to exist.

"Do not forget his arm, Dess." Meriah said, and even though the fabric was ripped enough to clearly see the four small slashes in his arm, he rolled up his sleeve so Destiny could see it better.

"How are you with bruises?" Conner asked, lifting up his shirt to reveal a rather large patch of purple skin where Dante had kicked him in the stomach. Destiny instantly felt bad for having poked him there to wake him up. He winced when Destiny just came close, and she told him everything was going to be fine because she didn't have to touch it in order to heal it. A minute later, the bruise had faded so that it too was no different than any other skin on him. "Much gratitude to you." he said gratefully as he lowered his shirt.

"You are most welcome." Destiny replied with a smile.

As Conner stood up, he wavered a moment, and almost fell, but Meriah stepped up and caught him. The jerking movement, however, sent something flying out of Conner's small pouch. Why Conner still had his pouch when no one else did, no one knew. Destiny noticed the object and picked it up. It was a small piece of paper, folded several times with the name "Conner" scrawled across the top of it. She handed it to Conner and his eyes grew wide as he realized whose handwriting it was. "Tis a note from Dante!" He gasped, and they all huddled around the small paper as he began to read...

Chapter Five

Jarron discovered that the lonely bartender's name was Sairynn. Since he had nothing left, he decided to join Jarron on his quest to find his brother. Maybe if they could find Axel, he could also find out what happened to his family. So they set off to find The Wizard by wandering through the woods. If anyone knew what was going on, it would be him. They gathered up some supplies before they left, and spent three days meandering through the trees before anything really happened. On the third day, not long after they set out in the morning, they saw a sign. A sign made of stone that had a name carved into it. And the name was The Wizard.

This was not the small cave that Axel had found. Before them loomed a magnificent stone castle, nestled here in the middle of the forest, looking very out of place with all the greenery surrounding it. Around the edges of the castle was a moat, with only one bridge. The bridge, however, was not down, leaving a rather large river of water between them and their target.

The two companions looked at each other uncertainly. "Can you swim?" Jarron asked. Sairynn shook his head slowly. Jarron smiled slightly and said, "Neither can I."

The two thought it over for a minute. "It's really not very far." Sairynn commented. Jarron could tell by the look on his face that he was hatching a plan.

"What are you thinking?" Jarron asked.

Sairynn did not respond for a moment. Then he turned slowly to face Jarron. "Well, all we really need is something that floats, and is big enough to support us. I was thinking, if we each found a big enough log, it might be enough just to keep us above the water. Then we just kick like crazy until we make it to the other side."

"Do you really think that will work?" Jarron asked doubtfully.

"I do not know. But it cannot hurt to try." Sairynn replied.

Jarron turned around and went back into the woods, and brought back the biggest branch that he could. Using all the strength he could, he dragged the large branch to the water and chucked it in. As predicted, it stayed afloat above the water. Jarron took a deep breath and jumped in after it. His left arm hooked the log, sinking it under a bit with the force of the blow. His arm was also suffering from the impact, but no real harm was done. The log worked to keep him from drowning, and that was good enough. His feet could not feel the bottom, so he guessed it was pretty deep. Jarron was about to start kicking when Sairynn yelled for him to wait.

"Here, take this." Sairynn said, opening his pouch of supplies and throwing Jarron a rope. "Tie it around the end so that I can drag it back here once you are across."

Jarron did as he was instructed and then began to kick his legs madly in an attempt to get across the river. At first it seemed to have no effect. So Jarron pulled himself up a little more so that he was almost parallel with the water. This worked much better. Jarron was across the river in a matter of minutes. Getting his feet planted safely on solid ground again was a bit more difficult, but he accomplished this too after a couple of tries.

When at last Sairynn joined him on the other side, they turned to face the castle. They didn't know where to start. One does not simply walk up to a castle and knock on the door. But what other choice did they have? Two men pounding on a giant wooden door to a stone castle in the middle of nowhere don't really have much chance of being heard by anyone. But maybe if they used the wooden branch...

Jarron ran back to the moat and tried to grab the log. Sairynn came to help, but they were still having trouble grasping the wood well enough to haul it back to the shore.

"What are you two doing?" The log splashed back into the water, drenching the already wet Jarron and Sairynn. They jumped to attention, spinning around to face the newcomer.

He was a bit younger than Jarron, probably around Axel's age. He was tall and thin, and did not seem very threatening at all. His black greasy hair fell to his shoulders and his dark brown eyes held a look of suspicion as he looked the two intruders over.

Jarron did not know what to say. They certainly could not tell him that they were trying to break into the castle. He'd probably have them killed. Before he could think of anything, Sairynn spoke up. "We were looking for The Wizard."

He raised an eyebrow at them. "Have you been summoned?"

Jarron and Sairynn looked at each other uncertainly. "...Yes?"

"It is not wise to lie to me, Jarron."

Both of the men's mouths dropped open slightly. How did he know Jarron's name? *Could he be The Wizard?* No, impossible. He was just a kid. But then again, The Wizard is all powerful and all knowing, so why wouldn't he know their names? And why wouldn't he would have the power to make himself look younger? He was said to be immortal after all, so he had to keep himself going somehow.

The stranger laughed. "I am not The Wizard, but I do work for him." He smiled mischievously. "My name is Vincent. Vincent Black." He held out his hand, but Jarron was still too shocked to shake hands. How had he known what he was thinking? Sairynn took the initiative and tentatively grabbed Vincent's hand. "Well, come on. You will not get in that way. Follow me." He grinned and spun around a little too quickly before darting off around the castle. Jarron and Sairynn looked at each other uncertainly. Sairynn shrugged his shoulders. They figured they had no other choice but to follow him.

*****

When Dante awoke, he looked around and became aware of the fact that the tavern was gone and so were most of the people in it. It had been replaced by what appeared to be a giant dirt pit. There were only four other bodies lying here with him; those of Conner and his friend, and two girls that looked only vaguely familiar to him. Then a sudden realization dawned on him: someone was missing. "Katara!" He yelled her name in vain, for she was nowhere in sight. He jumped to his feet and yelled for her again, his eyes monitoring the entire area around him. No luck. Nothing but dirt and a few trees.

Where was he anyway? It seemed to be some kind of ravine in the middle of a forest. But which forest? What town was close by, if any? The trees looked so very high above him, and so very far away. Had Katara really climbed all of that on her own? No, he didn't think so. Besides, she wouldn't just leave him. Not after all they'd been through together. It just wasn't like her. She was loyal, just like he was to her.

A dark thought crossed Dante's mind: The king. If that bloody king had done anything to hurt her... His hand automatically went to his hilt, and then he found out that Katara wasn't the only thing missing. His beautiful swords were gone. Both of them. Dante swore. Now he was really upset. If he ever found that king again... His anger welled up inside of him, but deep down he knew that that's all it would ever do. He knew that he would never get the revenge he always dreamed of, never strike back at the one who tortured him, never stand up and fight for his own freedom. That was not the case, however, when it came to Katara. He would do anything for her, and stand up to the wildest, most deadly beast to save her. If that beast was the king, then so be it. He would give his own life if it meant saving hers.

Dante sighed. What was he going to do? He had to find Katara, but then there was also Conner. He looked down at his still sleeping form, somehow looking so peaceful even though he was in the middle of a pile of twigs and leaves. Dante knew as soon as he did wake that he would be majorly freaking out about how badly his hair was getting messed up. A smile slowly creeped across Dante's face as he remembered fun times he used to have with his old friend. His best friend, at some points, his only friend at others. He never meant to hurt him. Never. He wanted to apologize; to explain. He knelt down beside Conner's slumbering form and tried desperately to shake him awake, but to no avail. Next he tried yelling as loud as he could, right in his face, but nothing helped. Whatever spell the king had put on them could only be removed on his terms when he wanted, it seemed. Dante exhaled in anxiety. He didn't have much time. He had to find Katara. There was no telling what kind of horrors could be threatening her. He had to get to her; to protect her.

It was amazing that he was actually thinking clearly. Even though he could feel the darkness pulling on him since the moment he had woken up, he resisted the urge to give in. The darkness took over his mind like a drug, and he often had blackouts where it had so completely taken over his mind that he had no idea what had happened for the past several hours, or however long it had had such a very strong hold over him.

Not sure what else to do, he got out a quill and a piece of old parchment from the pocket of his long jacket and began to scrawl a message to his friend. He kept the message short, and he wrote as quickly as he could, for he knew that this momentary sanity wouldn't last long. He shook his head to try to clear it. Just a little while longer. He had to try to help Conner before he was forced to destroy him. He wrote an apology, and he knew it all probably sounded insane, but if Conner was still the same old man as he used to be so many years ago, he would understand. Dante prayed that he was, and that he would accept his warning, and take his friends far away from him. He was dangerous. He hated to admit it, but it was true. To not have control over your own thoughts, your own actions, is a very dangerous thing indeed. He prayed that Conner would listen to his warning.

When he finished writing the note, he folded it, wrote Conner's name on the top of it, and tucked it into the small pouch that was hanging off of Conner's belt. Then he got up and ran to the closest edge and started to climb out of the pit. Normally he would just transport from one spot to another, and save himself the hard labor of climbing up such a steep slope, but in a place he had never seen before, it was very difficult and rather risky to try teleportation. No one wants to reappear in the middle of a tree or something and be forever stuck half-in and half-out. Besides, he had to keep his senses keen at all times for any sign of Katara.

As soon as he got to the top of the hill, Dante called out for Katara again. Still no luck. He looked around, wondering which direction to start his search for her. After a while, he heard a rustling coming from down in the pit. He decided he better get out of there before the others awoke, so he ran as fast as he could into the unknown.

Chapter Six

"I do not understand. Why does his master want you dead?" asked Axel, as Conner had finished reading the note. "And who *is* his master, anyway?"

Conner did not reply at first. He just stood there, rereading the letter silently to himself. "I do not know." Conner replied slowly. He was lying, and he hated lying to Axel. He hoped that it didn't show on his face. Oh, yes, Conner knew. Conner had caught Dante's hidden meaning in the note. But that was not to be discussed until later. Much later. Why he wanted Conner dead was of little importance. All that mattered was keeping Axel safe. And that was exactly what Conner planned on doing.

"I will teach you a little magic if you wish." Destiny said, trying to lighten the mood.

"She really is quite magnificent at healing." Meriah chimed in, smiling up at him encouragingly.

"Tis a basic art." Destiny said, brushing the compliment aside.

"No, really, you really are quite wonderful at that." Conner cut in, examining his hands and his arm where the wounds used to be.

Destiny smiled, and actually blushed a bit. "Thank you kindly." She mumbled, "Although, 'twas nothing really... Quite basic..." It was one thing when your sister told you were good; that was to be expected (and she had heard it from her a thousand and one times), but when someone you've only just met says it, *then* it actually means something. Destiny felt a sense of pride growing inside of her (another thing that it was improper for a woman to have) as Conner smiled kindly at her.

Axel sighed. "Indeed, to learn magic would be greatly befitting, nevertheless first we must rid ourselves of Dante."

Destiny turned toward Axel and crossed her arms. Meriah recognized that look: she was fuming inside and about to blow up with whatever it was that was on her mind. "Destiny, remember your place." she told her in a hushed warning tone.

Reluctantly, Destiny kept her mouth shut. It was a very difficult thing for her to do, however. It was against her nature. She wanted to be wild and free and to not have to live by society's rules or have to care what was proper and what was not. Axel was a fool, and she wanted to let him know it! He had destroyed her happy moment and she was furious about it. The nerve of him! How very stupid men can be! Of course she had suggested learning magic as a way to best their enemies. Did he really think she would go through all that hard training with someone just for fun? Was he seriously going to reject the chance to learn magic when it could be his only hope to win against an unknown adversary? What if that big king guy was still lurking around somewhere? If that selfish codfish Axel doesn't have his precious weaponry, or any form of magic, how can he even think he can stand up against someone who just knocked them out for 900 some odd years without even laying a hand on any of them? Who knows what kind of other powers he could have! Not to mention that he was about seven feet tall and wide as can be! What kind of idiot was this Axel? Wasn't it obvious that magic was their only hope?

Perhaps this was the wrong guy after all. He sure as heck didn't seem like the mighty "dragon" that The Wizard had called him. Unless of course he meant the fact that his ignorance and annoyance were as beastly as a dragon. That would be completely correct. This is most definitely the right guy.

Well, if he didn't want her help it was his loss. Perhaps The Wizard had made a mistake. It wouldn't be the first time. Why would he send her and her sister to help Axel? It was impossible. He was too much of a thick-skulled, arrogant, contemptuous harpy to be helped! It was like trying to help the whole ocean fit into one small glass. Preposterous!

Oh, what was to become of their mission? They were not even sure what it was. All The Wizard told them was to assist Axel and Conner on their journey. But what journey was that? Perhaps it might be a good idea to go find The Wizard. Seek his knowledge; his wisdom; his advice. He would know what to do. The Wizard knows everything. But where was he, and where were they? This town looked nothing like Shyloh, and how were they to know which direction to even start looking for the cave in the woods if they had no idea where they were to begin with?

There was something bigger going on here. Bigger than all of them. The Wizard must have known it. He had sent them to the Bent Tree Limb in order to meet up with each other and then the king had sent them all here. Had the king interfered with The Wizard's plans, or was he just a smaller part in the bigger picture; a stepping stone to get them where they needed to go?

Everything happens for a reason. Of that, Destiny was absolutely sure. So she decided that this was where their mission must be, and these two men must be the right ones. It was no accident that they all had been knocked out together. Besides, if The Wizard is really all-knowing, then that means he willingly sent them here, and he wouldn't send them to their doom. He sent them here to face whatever their mission was, and to face it together. He knew it would take all of them to complete this mission, and that was why they were here.

The Wizard wouldn't sentence them to their death. He knew they could do it... right? Really, not much was known about The Wizard, but most people said he was good. Everyone knows of his great and wonderful powers, but after all, one can be great and still be evil.

Dante didn't seem too trustworthy a character himself. First he's trying to kill Conner and now he's playing nice? Destiny didn't buy it. Not for a second. Why would he write him a letter like that? He was still going to go back to his master, and he was still going to try to kill Conner, so what was the point? What was this "darkness" that he spoke of? Could one actually control another's thoughts, actions even, just by using dark magic? Destiny had heard of such things, long ago, but had always disregarded them as legends; fantasies; stories that parents told their children to scare them into being good. She had never once ever considered the fact that they could be true. If he really was being controlled by such a power, then how had he had the sanity to write the letter in the first place? It all seemed a bit dodgy to her, and she didn't trust him.

"The sun is setting." Conner said, interrupting Destiny's thoughts. "Let us find a safe place to rest for the night."

"Perhaps there is a church nearby." Meriah said, "If not to stay, surely they will direct us to a better place."

"Tis a marvelous idea." Conner said, smiling at her. "I shall go and search for one."

"No, we know nothing of this place. It would not be wise for you to go alone, Conner." said Destiny, putting her hand on his arm to stop him from walking away.

"She's right." said Axel, hating to admit it. "We may never find each other again if we split up."

So they followed the road for many miles. They left the woods far behind, and they saw nothing but houses on either side of them. Most of them looked pretty much the same. Any people who saw them stopped and stared. The four of them stared at the people here almost as much as they stared at them. They walked around with barely anything on! Few of the guys wore shirts, a fact that wasn't too uncommon (and that Destiny loved very much), but their woman! They walked around in pants like men! And some of them looked as if they were wearing less than their undergarments. Have they no decency here? Not that Axel really minded all the extra skin showing, but it was just such a shock to see them walking around so nonchalantly like it was the most normal thing in the world. It had long since gone dark, but their way was lit up by these magical poles that grew up out of the ground following the road. A small light shone at the top of each of these poles, and led them finally to a small church.

"It's small, but it will do." said Axel, looking the place over the best he could in the dim light of the magical poles. It was rather small, but cozy looking place. The type of place where everybody knew everybody and there were always happy, smiling faces. At least it looked that way from the outside.

Destiny rolled her eyes at him. *Why is nothing ever good enough for some men?* "Just be happy you have a place to stay at all." *You ungrateful little prat!* She added in her head.

The church however, was most obviously closed, and they tried every door they could find to get in, but it was no use. They were going to have to camp out on the ground. Again. Axel sat down on the ground and rested his back against the brick wall. Conner sat down next to him, with Destiny beside him, and Meriah on the far end. Before they knew it, Conner was passed out leaning on Axel, Destiny was leaning on Conner, and Meriah was leaning on her sister.

Axel had been pushed so far over he was now laying at a weird angle on the hard ground.

*****

Vincent led the way around the great stone castle to a hidden door on the back side. He pushed away the vines that covered it, and effortlessly pushed open the door despite its considerable weight. Jarron wondered why someone who worked for The Wizard would have to be so secret when entering his own workplace, but then his incredible strength drove that thought from his mind. This Vincent guy really wasn't much to look at. He was pale and skinny, and if anyone asked, Jarron would probably say that he was a young weakling. How was it then that he could so easily push aside a door twice his size?

"So, what is it that you guys want to know?" Vincent asked, not looking at them. He was leading them down a very dark hallway. Sairynn and Jarron could barely see a foot in front of them, but Vincent seemed to be able to navigate perfectly despite the absence of light. They assumed it was because he was used to the place and knew his way around.

Sairynn started to explain about the fight that destroyed his pub, and the strange way that everyone disappeared. Jarron cut in only to add that his brother had been there in the fight and had also vanished. "To put it simply, we just want to know how to get our families back." Sairynn finished.

Vincent listened to their story but said nothing. He led them to a large waiting room that was so brightly lit that Jarron and Sairynn had to shield their eyes as they entered. The change in lighting did not seem to effect Vincent. "Wait here." He instructed, gesturing to some comfortable looking benches. With inhuman speed, Vincent was suddenly at the other end of the room, and then he blended in with the darkness and was lost from their sight.

Vincent ran down the hallways, not looking for The Wizard but someone else entirely. He hadn't completely lied to the newcomers; he did work for The Wizard. Once. He had messed up and was afraid to come back for fear that The Wizard would kill him. But now The Wizard had something of his. And he wasn't about to give it up without a fight. He thought about Jarron and Sairynn waiting patiently back in the grand hall. How long should he leave them there? He would have to come get them eventually. If they tried to stop him from escaping, well, he could dispose of them easy enough.

He wondered briefly what he would do if he actually ran into The Wizard. Would he be able to conquer him as easily as the others? Even after ten years of working for The Wizard, Vincent still had no idea what he looked like. No one did. He wondered if he was invisible. He had only ever heard his voice. His loud, grating, vexatious voice. Telling him what to do. What not to do. Who to bless. Who to curse. Vincent was tired of his life being dictated by someone else. He was going to take back what was his if it was the last thing he ever did.

Jarron and Sairynn were intensely bored. They had been sitting here waiting for what seemed like hours. Jarron started nodding off to sleep. Sairynn quickly followed. They had no idea how long they'd been there sleeping when a thunderous voice filled the room, paralyzing them in fear. They sat up, instantly awake and alert.

"WHY HAST THOU INVADED MY CASTLE?"

Sairynn and Jarron jumped up off the bench, trying to find the source of the voice, but it seemed to be coming from everywhere at once. It would appear that they were alone in the room, and yet the voice boomed again: "THOU ART TRESPASSING. EXPLAIN, OR FACE MY WRATH!"

"W-we are sorry, sir." Sairynn spoke up. When he got no response, he decided to go ahead and explain the whole story. When he was finished, it seemed as though the voice was not going to respond at all. He looked over at Jarron, who held the same look of confusion as Sairynn did. Sairynn was just about to comment on how nice it was to not have the exceedingly loud voice trying to break their eardrums with its extraordinarily deafening noise when the voice spoke again.

"THE PEOPLE THAT THOU SEEKETH HATH GONE WHERE THOU CANST NOT FOLLOW."

Neither Jarron nor Sairynn liked that answer. It told them nothing, and certainly didn't help them to find Axel or anyone else. It was Jarron's turn to speak up. He took a deep breath and said with defiance, "We are prepared to follow them no matter where they have gone. If you know where-"

"THE WIZARD HAS NOTHING MORE TO SAY. LEAVE NOW, AND THOU SHALT REMAIN UNHARMED."

Jarron and Sairynn exchanged weary looks. What should they do? They couldn't just give up and go home. Not when everyone Sairynn knew was gone along with Axel and his goofy friend. No, they had to do something. Jarron took a few steps forward towards the center of the room and planted his feet firmly on the ground. He looked a lot braver than he felt. He took a deep breath to steady himself, and then said, "We are not leaving until we have our families back."

As if in response, the ground began to shake. There was a great rumble as if thunder was rolling all around them. Jarron almost lost his footing. Sairynn did. His efforts to get back up all proved to be pointless, and so he just stopped trying. The earthquake did not stop, however. The solid floor beneath their feet began to crack. Before they knew it, there was a hole in the floor separating Jarron and Sairynn.

"Sairynn! Quickly! Jump!"

Sairynn could barely get to his feet let alone jumping over an ever growing crater between them. It was just then that the guy named Vincent returned.

"What did you guys do?!" He asked. He had never seen The Wizard this mad about anything. He was destroying his castle! If they were all still inside when it collapsed...

"We have got to get out of here. This place is not going to last long." Jarron and Sairynn both turned to see where the new voice came from. It was a woman's voice, and it sounded very beautiful. Her voice, however, did not do justice to the real thing. She was gorgeous. She had long, elegant ringlets in her reddish-brown hair, and fascinating sapphire eyes. And Jarron knew exactly who she was.

"Rebecca?" Jarron asked in disbelief.

"No time for chit-chat, Jair, if we do not leave soon, we are all going to die."

Vincent didn't care much for the two people he brought in here. He just wanted to get Rebecca and get out. Sairynn was still on the other side of the cavern, and had lost all hope of ever getting across. Rebecca wasn't about to leave anyone behind. With amazing speed, she darted directly at the cliff. Without stopping to even access how far the jump was, she leaped across the hole, landing safely and sturdily on the other side, despite the shaking ground. She scooped up Sairynn in her arms and ran at the canyon again. Sairynn was scared to death, not that he'd ever admit it. To make matters worse, he was just saved by a girl. An amazingly athletic and unbelievably graceful girl, but a girl just the same. Rebecca did not give Sairynn a chance to stand up on his own. She bounded over the chasm and kept right on going. She was halfway down the dark hallway before Jarron even turned to follow.

Chapter Seven

Destiny was the first to wake up in the morning. She realized her head was resting most comfortably on Conner's arm, and so she pretended to still be asleep so she could stay like that just a little while longer. Unfortunately, Axel woke up next, and when he moved everyone else did too. They fell like dominoes on top of one another, and Conner hit his head hard on the ground. For once he was interested in something other than his hair when he woke up. The side of his head was bleeding a bit, and of course, he started to freak out about it. Destiny told him to stop being such a baby and swiftly healed the tiny cut.

"Uhm... Can I help you guys?" The four of them looked up to see a man standing over them with a look of confusion on his face. He was an average man, not too short, not too tall, with dark hair and eyes. He wore a plain black t-shirt and blue jeans. There was a teenage girl standing a little way behind him.

Axel stood up to greet the newcomer. "Hello, kind sir. My name is Axel, and these are my friends, Conner, Destiny, and Meriah. We are travelers from..." Axel debated whether or not he should tell the pastor that they were from the past, and decided he'd save that story for later. Right now they really just needed some shelter and food. They didn't want to scare him away with their fantastic tale of time-traveling magic. Not yet, anyway. "...from a very distant land, and we were wondering if we might be able to rest awhile in your church."

He looked at each one of them in turn, taking in their clothes, the fact that they were filthy dirty, and that they didn't smell very good. He didn't know which was worse: Conner with his ripped knees and dried blood everywhere, or the fact that Destiny's dress was just a piece of material being held up by a rope. He glanced over at the girl that was with him to take in her reaction. She looked just about as stumped and bewildered as he was. He thought for a moment and then decided that the right thing to do would be to let them inside.

He took out a key and unlocked the door, holding it open for everyone to get inside. The teenage girl came in last, exchanging a questioning look with the man holding the door open.

As Axel, Conner, Destiny, and Meriah walked through the door they were amazed by all the strange things that surrounded them. To their left was an odd metal-looking structure attached to the wall that appeared to be some sort of fountain, but there was no water coming out of it. To their right was a very nice area for hanging up their jackets. As they walked a little farther into the church, they saw two rooms with signs on the doors. The first one read "WOMEN" and the second "MEN". The travelers were intrigued by these doors, and wondered greatly what lay behind them, especially since they were separated into male and female only rooms. To the rest of the group's great disappointment, the man led them right past the mysterious rooms, and the benches that were across from them, to a rather large room on the left with large glass windows. He pushed open the door, and walked inside.

"This is our sanctuary." He explained. Please, make yourselves at home." He paused for a minute, then added, "How rude of me, I've forgotten to introduce myself. My name is Chad, and I am the pastor here. This is my daughter, Jacquelynn." He said, indicating the teenage girl that was with him. She had an odd haircut, it was much longer in the front and very short in the back. It was a darker black color than any of them had ever seen, and it really helped to make her blue eyes shine. She also had black make-up around her eyes, and very long, beautiful eyelashes. She had nothing of her father's plainness, except perhaps his nose. Her face was very beautiful, even though she dressed in pants like a boy. It would take them all a very long time to get used to the new dress code around here.

"Dad, *please*." The girl said, rolling her eyes. "Call me Jack."

"Alright, Jackie." He smiled and she rolled her eyes at him again. Then he turned to face the four new strangers. "I'll be right back. I have to call my wife to tell her I won't be home tonight."

"Do you want me to yell for her?" asked Conner. "I can be very loud."

Pastor Chad laughed. "I'm sure you can, but that's alright. I'll just use the phone. Besides, I don't think she'll hear you from here." He laughed again as he walked away.

"Well, if you are sure." said Conner, "Let me know if you need help!"

Meriah turned to her sister. "What is a phone?" she asked. Destiny shrugged her shoulders, just as lost as the rest of them.

"Seriously, are you guys for real?" Jack asked as soon as her father had left. The only response she got was four blank faces staring back at her. "Where did you say you were from?"

"Conner and I live in the small town called Salbris." Axel answered her.

"My sister and I are from Shyloh. Do you happen to know how far we are from Shyloh?" asked Destiny.

"I've never heard of Shyloh. Or Salbris. What state is it in?"

"State?" asked Destiny, looking around to the others for help. "I do not really know; I have not been there in over 900 years."

Jack laughed. "You guys are funny."

Axel rolled his eyes. "We do not have time for this. We need to figure out what we are going to do about Sinclaire and that fire hazard."

"His name is Dante." Conner mumbled, slightly annoyed by Axel's refusal to address Dante by his first name.

"Who's Dante?" Jack asked, her interest peeked.

"Well, it is kind of a long story..." Axel started.

Before he could get any farther into his explanation, Pastor Chad came back and interrupted him. Jack told him to stay quiet and he apologized.

"As I was saying," Axel continued after giving Chad a sharp glance that clearly stated his annoyance at being interrupted. "It all started when my cow turned up missing the other day, and-"

"Enough with the cow." Cut in Destiny, "It all started when we all got called to see The Wizard..."

Chad and his daughter listened to their story with great interest. Everyone cut in to tell their part. Especially Conner. He went on about *his* important mission that *he* got directly from The Wizard. Everyone laughed, even Pastor Chad.

"So that's what happened." Axel said as he finished telling Chad what had *really* happened.

Chad clearly didn't believe a word of what they said, he found it all a bit far-fetched and impossible. He decided to humor them anyway. "Well, you guys must be hungry. Let's go see what we have in the fridge."

While the four of them tried to figure out what in the world a fridge could be, they followed Pastor Chad and Jack through the halls of the church. Jack was very excited and was asking them a million questions, without even giving them time to answer. At one point they passed a bunch of glass cases with some old artifacts in them.

"My sword!" Axel exclaimed, recognizing the silver double-edged beauty the moment he saw it. At last, he would be complete again. How perfectly she fit into his hands. She was long and thin and extremely sharp. Wrapped around her handle was a black dragon. The dragon's head was on the pommel, its mouth open and teeth bared. It's red ruby eyes glistened in the low light. The dragon's body went down the hilt, and its tail wrapped around the top part of the blade. This was his father's sword. His most prized possession. The most beautiful piece of weaponry that Axel had ever seen. The only thing that stood between him and his weapon was a thin piece of glass. And the pastor named Chad.

"What?" Chad, who had not been paying attention to any of the rest of their conversation, stopped and turned around at the mention of a sword.

"And my bow!" Conner was so excited to see his bow and pouch full of arrows he completely lost all interest in everything else and drifted off into pleasant memories of so long ago when he had first made his bow. He picked out the wood and shaped it, attached the string, and then set out to hand-craft the arrows. It was one of his most prized possessions, and he loved it dearly. His bow was more than just a weapon. It was a friend. A friend with whom he had been inseparable before he had been lost. He had poured countless hours into making it perfect, and thought it looked rather majestic sitting there behind glass being displayed proudly for all to see. Even so, he could not help but feel sad for his old friend. How lonely it must be, to be locked inside a display case for the rest of your life, with no one to hold you, hunt with you, or just play around the training field trying to hit some bullseyes with you. Conner wanted to apologize, try to make him see that he hadn't abandoned him. He wanted to tell his friend how he had been brought here against his will, and never, ever, would he have left him behind. Then he had to remind himself that his bow was, after all, only an inanimate object that didn't really have any feelings and so therefore could not have possibly been hurt by their separation. He was still trying to convince himself of this fact when the sound of breaking glass penetrated into his mind and broke his train of thought.

Apparently, Chad had denied Axel his sword, and Axel wasn't about to take no for an answer. Chad insisted that it was impossible for that sword to be his seeing as the sword was older than the church itself, which was built over 100 years ago. Axel countered that the sword itself was forged over 900 years ago, and passed down from generation to generation through his family. He even went on to tell him about how his father had given it to him as he lay dying in his sickbed. When Chad still refused to believe him, Axel decided he would simply take back what was his.

Jack screamed out in horror as Axel's fist flew at full speed right into the heart of the glass display case that held his sword captive. Axel didn't seem to notice the blood now oozing out of several places on his hand, or the little shards of glass that still clung on to him. He just wore a smug grin as he reached in with both hands and ever-so-gently took out his sword. He inspected every inch of the weapon, flicking off a few flecks of dust and dirt here and there, before placing the sword back into its rightful place at his side.

Chad was so overcome with rage he didn't know what to say. Not only had he destroyed church property, but stealing a precious artifact older than the church itself? How dare he! Who did he think he was? What kind of person walks into a church and puts their fist through a glass case? How dare he waltz into God's house and destroy it? It wasn't really about the glass case, or what was inside it, it was the principle of the matter. Here he thought he was doing the right thing by letting them in and he was going to feed them and everything, and this is how they repay him? He'd had enough. They'd get no food and they'd get no more hospitality. They were leaving. Now.

Destiny, while irritated with Axel for being such a giant baby about not getting his way, had busied herself with trying to pick the glass out of Axel's hand before healing it. Which was rather difficult with him waving it around in anger while arguing with the indignant Pastor Chad.

Meanwhile no one seemed to notice Conner gradually creeping closer to the now ruined case, where he gingerly picked up his bow and, in slow motion, placed his pack of cherished arrows gently on his back. As his fingers brushed the fine wood of his beloved bow, he felt feelings of joy and cheer rushing into him. A chill ran through his whole body as feelings so exhilarating to his soul filled up his entire being. At last, he was whole again. He held the bow in both his hands and just stared at it, losing track of all time and everything that was going on around him.

Meriah had been quiet throughout most of this incident, letting out only a very faint gasp when Axel's fist first met the glass. It all happened so very quickly and there was nothing anyone could have done to prevent it. There wasn't much they could do to fix it either. Meriah knew it was her place to be silent, especially where men are concerned. Not to mention that one of them was the leader of the church, and that he should have ultimate authority over all of them. No one was ever supposed to argue with a priest. Whatever he said came from God, and God is always right. While Axel didn't seem to care a bit about most likely damning his soul to eternal torture in the lakes of fire that make up Hell, Meriah chose to stay silent, and pray. She prayed that Chad's eyes would be opened to the truth of who they really were, and that he would forgive Axel for his destructive rudeness. She prayed that they would have a place to stay for the night, even if it wasn't here, and she prayed to at least have one small meal before going to bed on what she was sure to be a very long day. All of her prayers were not needs, however. She praised God that they had made it this far, and praised him for sending the bear to fill their bellies. She praised God for Chad and his church, for letting them in, even if it was only for a little while. She thanked the Lord for her sister's healing abilities, and as was her normal routine, she asked the Lord to show her the way to righteousness, to show her how to behave properly, and perhaps someday she might find a man brave enough to put up with her for the rest of his life.

Pastor Chad was determined to kick them out of the church, but Jack was trying her best to calm him down. She wanted to let them stay, hear more of their story, and help them in any way she could. She didn't know what it was that made her believe them so whole-heartedly, perhaps it was God himself trying to tell her that they were good people, but something inside of her just knew that they were telling the truth. Why else would they be dressed the way they are? Smelling the way they do? Covered in dirt, and some in blood? Why make up a whole story, why not just say they were homeless or something? It was obvious they didn't come in intending to do any damage. Axel was shocked when he saw his sword, and he just wanted to get back what was rightfully his. True, his methods were not the greatest, but it was *his* sword. If they were to keep it, then didn't that make *them* the thieves? Her father just didn't seem to understand. How could she convince him to let them stay? Her case was made all the more difficult when Destiny started healing Axel's hand.

When she had finally picked out all the glass she could see, Destiny held Axel's hand in both of hers and started the healing process. It only took a few seconds to finish, the cuts were small and not very deep, but that small action raised a whole other argument and turned Chad even farther away from them. Destiny could not understand why he was upset with her. If God has granted you the power to heal someone, are you not supposed to use it? Didn't Jesus himself heal people? Why was it such a big deal for her to use magic in the church? It's not like she was using any dark magic; she was only helping a friend in need.

"Dad, can I talk to you for a minute?" Jack interrupted her thoughts, dragging her father away to speak with him. Destiny had no idea what she said to him, but it worked. When they returned, Pastor Chad had calmed down, and agreed to let them stay for as long as they needed to.

From that point on, Jack was one of their best friends.

Reluctantly, Chad made them a small meal, and found them some blankets to use for the night. He then went into his office and tried to busy himself with his paperwork that he had come there to do. No matter how hard he tried, he couldn't concentrate. He knew Jack was out there with those delirious teenagers and it just didn't seem safe. He didn't trust them. They were obviously mental patients. Perhaps he should call the hospital and see if anybody escaped lately. He put down his pencil and stared at his phone. No, Jack was right. He needed to show them mercy and grace, and treat them as he would want to be treated. Do what Jesus would do. Turn the other cheek. Forgive them seventy times seven times in a day. It was just so very hard sometimes.

Silently Meriah thanked the Lord for Pastor Chad and his kindness. In just a short amount of time her prayers had been answered. She praised God and thanked him before sitting down and enjoying her food.

Chad debated whether or not he should stay the night with them. He wasn't sure if he trusted them enough to leave them here by themselves. He certainly didn't trust them around Jack. His eyes bore into his phone again, and he wondered just how long he had been sitting there staring at it. Then he heard a loud noise and his heart immediately leapt into his throat. He stood up a little too quickly and almost knocked over his chair. He took a second to steady it before running out the door. There was a sound of footsteps approaching, although he couldn't really hear them over the sound of his heart beating so loudly in his ears. He ran down the hallway that led to the sanctuary, and reached out to open the door.

The door opened before he touched it. Jack was on the other side, and ran right into her father. She laughed and asked him why he was in such a hurry.

Not wanting to seem like a fool for being all worked up over nothing, Chad made up his mind to go ahead and send his daughter home. Better to be safe than sorry. "I was coming to tell you that I'm going to call your mother to come get you... and that I'll be spending the night here and watching over our... friends."

Jack's face fell in disappointment. "Dad, why can't I stay?"

"You'll be safer at home, Jacquelynn." Chad said sternly.

"*Dad.*" Jack protested at both the unfairness of the situation and the use of her full name. She could tell that he wasn't going to budge on the subject. Besides, she didn't want to push him too far or he might change his mind about them altogether. Jack sighed and slumped down onto a bench as her father got out his cell phone to make the call.

"So what were you coming to tell me, Jackie?" Chad asked her when he was done with his phone.

"What? Oh, just that Destiny and Meriah and the guys are tired, and they were going to bed." Jack answered grumpily. Why must he always treat her like a child? She was 16 now, almost 17. She could take care of herself. She wasn't afraid of the newcomers; she was fascinated by them. They weren't there to hurt them; they were just lost. They just needed help. If they didn't help them, who would? As crazy as it sounded, what if everything they said was true? What if there really was an evil king after them? And a girl that could shoot fire from her hands? If nothing else, they needed a place to hide. A place where they would be safe.

The sound of her mother's car pulling into the driveway caught her attention just then, and she got up to leave. Before she got to the door, she turned around to face her dad. "Will I at least get to see them again tomorrow?"

"I don't know, Jackie. You have school in the morning. I want you to get some sleep tonight. Now go on, your mother's waiting." He gestured towards the door where he could see his wife was waiting in the car. Jack sighed and rolled her eyes at him before walking outside and getting in the car.

*****

Rebecca didn't set down Sairynn until they were outside and on the other side of the moat. Vincent reluctantly grabbed Jarron and easily leaped over the moat, dropping him none-too-gently on the other side. They watched in awe as the magnificent castle they had just been in began to crumble to the ground. Within a few minutes the grand structure was nothing more than a giant pile of rubble. Jarron couldn't believe it. What the heck had just happened? As he stared at the debris of the castle, he ran over the whole scenario again in his head. None of it seemed to add up. First, the fact that no one knew where The Wizard lived. Everyone who went to see him came back with a different story. A great stone castle in a clearing in the middle of the woods is kind of obvious. Even though it was surrounded by a moat, what was to keep it from being discovered? He and Sairynn had found it easily enough after all.

Vincent was the second thing that didn't make sense. He claimed to be working for The Wizard, yet not even he could walk through the front gate to the castle. He had to creep around to a hidden entrance on the side, not to mention the incredible strength it took just to open the door. Once inside, he did not wait with them or bring The Wizard to them. He just left them abruptly, and then returned with Rebecca. Which brings up the next crazy thing that had happened: Rebecca. Everything about her was different, except for the fact that she looked exactly the same as the last time he had seen her. She was the last person he expected to see, and then the way she leaped across the ever-growing crater to get to Sairynn and so easily hoisted him all the way to safety by jumping over the moat? And Vincent had followed her just as easily. Suddenly the fact that Jarron and Sairynn had used an over-sized log as a floatation device sounded very childish indeed.

"Relax." Vincent said, seeing how upset Jarron was, "We are not going to hurt you."

Neither Jarron nor Sairynn were comforted by these words.

"Let us all just sit down and take it easy for a bit, okay?" Said Rebecca, also trying to calm them down.

Jarron threw his arms up in the air in obvious frustration. "Take it easy?!" He exclaimed, "How can I take it easy when my brother is missing, The Wizard's palace has been destroyed, and my royal neighbor, who, might I add, has been missing even longer than Axel has, can now jump over moats?!"

Rebecca sighed and sat down on the grass outside what used to be The Wizard's castle, promising to explain everything that had happened since he had seen her last. When they were all seated, she began her story. She told them about how she ran away three years ago because her father wanted her to get married, and then how a vampire found her and turned her into what she was today. She spent most of her life in those three years training herself to be able to be around humans without killing them. So far, she was doing a pretty good job. She had only ever killed two humans before, and those were the unfortunate hunters that just happened to be passing by the day she was changed. She didn't mean to hurt them, she really didn't, but she just couldn't help herself. She was so unbearably thirsty, and instinct had just taken over. Since then she'd learned to just hold her breath around humans. She didn't need to breathe to survive, and when she didn't breathe she couldn't smell how intoxicating the fresh flowing veins of a human really were. It also made it easier if she ate something before meeting a human, that way her thirst was a little more manageable. Being locked up in the castle for as long as she was, however, she hadn't had a thing to eat in over a week. All this talking wasn't helping either. Half way through the story, she paused, and, unable to control her hunger any longer, excused herself, and ran away into the forest. The whole ordeal didn't take more than a few minutes, and when she had finished, she tried to wipe off her mouth and clean herself up as best she could before returning to the others.

Chapter Eight

"How can you guys think of sleep at a time like this?" complained Axel, "We are miles from home in a time we know nothing about, and, oh yea, there is a huge king out there somewhere that wants to kill me! I mean us," he corrected himself after getting a hello-what-about-me look from Destiny. "And we do not even know why!"

"It is pretty late." said Destiny, turning to face Axel. Conner and Meriah were sitting on the sanctuary floor a little way away, talking quietly. Each one of them had one of the blankets that Chad had brought, not leaving any for the rest of them. Destiny smiled and rolled her eyes at them. *Typical. I suppose I'll have to share one with my sister then.* She glanced over at Conner, taking in his thin, but very nicely built body and wondered if she could get away with sharing his blankets instead.

"I have got to get him first. It is our only chance." Axel said, bringing Destiny back into reality. She started to say his name, ready to tell him that they should all get some sleep so that they will be well rested and ready for whatever tomorrow might hold, but Axel didn't let her finish even the first word.

"I will kill him." He said with malice. He stared straight ahead, glaring at the back wall. No doubt he was picturing the dark king's face there as he spoke.

Destiny sighed, ready to go to sleep and trying to think of how to convince Conner to let her lay next to him. She knew she was being insensitive, but Axel's constant complaining was starting to annoy her. A lot of things annoyed her when she was tired. Couldn't it all just wait until tomorrow? "You will get your chance." She said, mostly trying to pacify him, "You should know better than anyone he would kill you in an instant if he got the chance. You're not strong enough to face him alone." She paused, waiting for a reply. When none came she added, "Especially if you have had no sleep. Now, come on-"

"You do not get it!" Axel exploded, interrupting her yet again, and causing the room go deadly quiet as everyone stopped what they were doing to stare at him. Destiny moaned to herself, knowing that he would not calm down and let them get to sleep anytime soon. She shifted her weight to get a bit more comfortable and prepared herself for a long, loud, whiny speech. "I cannot get stronger!" Axel continued, his voice echoing slightly in the vast sanctuary room. "I need magic! I have learned all I can with my sword."

Then it was Destiny's turn to interrupt. "Well I offered to teach you." She spat at him. She folded her arms and turned away from him. Every time he interrupted her, she got a little more angry. She was holding back, not saying all the things she wanted to. She could've gone on for hours about his rudeness alone.

"What could I possibly learn from a woman?" Axel shot back without thinking.

That was it. The final straw. Destiny exploded, her wrath pouring out uncontrollably at Axel. She didn't even give him a chance to reply. She told him exactly what she thought of him, and he sat there staring at her, mouth slightly agape, shocked that she could be so intimidating even though she was only a short little girl.

Concerned, Conner got up from where he was sitting and walked over to where Destiny was screaming her head off, and tried, not very successfully, to calm her down. Meriah followed him, also trying to soothe her sister.

Having no luck with Destiny, Conner leaned over to ask Axel what in the world he had said to her to make her so upset.

Axel, having regained his composure just crossed his arms and rolled his eyes, smiling as he replied, "Oh, she is just too stubborn to admit that she likes me." He laughed.

Destiny didn't think the statement was funny. She had heard what he said and she wasn't about to let him get away with it. She paused her ranting, and just stared at him angrily for a minute. She was surprised that he would say that, especially after all the things she just said about him, but she would never let him know it. She had to do something to get back at him; to have the final say; to win the argument. It was just the way she was. So she had to do the most drastic thing she could think of.

Instead of coming back at him with some witty comment, she turned abruptly away from him. She walked right up to Conner and roughly grabbed him by the shirt, pulling him closer to her, and then planted a kiss right on his lips. It wasn't an innocent peck either.

Conner was shocked and confused by what was going on, however, he wasn't in the least bit disappointed. After the initial surprise wore off, it didn't take Conner long to give in and kiss her back. Then just as suddenly as she had started, Destiny abruptly stopped and stormed off, without even a glance back at Axel to see his reaction. Conner was left bewildered once again, wanting more.

Axel looked just as stunned as Conner felt. He watched Destiny crisply march off, not believing what he had just seen.

Conner glanced over at Axel's face and had to turn away so he wouldn't see him grin. Axel's face was just priceless. He stood there with his mouth hanging slightly open, eyes wide, watching Destiny as she walked away. Conner had to suppress his laughter. Then Conner turned and saw Meriah's reaction. The smile immediately disappeared from his face. Meriah was startled, yes, but her face held a very different expression then the one on Axel's face. As Conner looked into her light blue eyes, he saw something else there. Behind the stunned look, there was one other emotion. She was hurt. She tried not to let it show, but it was growing harder by the second. Conner asked her if she was alright, and she lost it. She turned away from him as tears began to fall, and ran down the aisle, towards the front of the church. Without stopping, she pushed through the glass doors at the back of the sanctuary and ran out into the hallway. She paused only for a moment, deciding where to go. She didn't want to be followed. That's when she saw the door labeled "Women". Perfect. It was the only place she could go to be alone. So without further hesitation, she ran into the women's restroom and into one of the stalls. She spent the next hour or so in there, crying.

Destiny had no idea what the repercussions of her actions would be. She had acted in the heat of the moment, carrying on without thinking, like she so often does. She wanted to hurt Axel, not physically, but just something to make up for what he'd said to her. Needless to say, he'd struck a nerve. Destiny knew she was stubborn. She knew she was supposed to submit to men, listen to them, and do as they say. The problem came when men tried to look down on her. Not as an equal, but as someone who is less worthy then them, simply because she was a woman. True, that was the way of things where they came from, but that had never stopped Destiny before. She was a free spirit. She didn't listen to anyone, except perhaps her sister on rare occasion. She had her own opinions of how things should be, and she wasn't afraid to let anyone know it. Man or woman. So when Axel had made the comment about not being able to learn from her simply because she was a woman, it had set her off. And then whispering to Conner and laughing at her had only fueled the fire. Any chance she had about being able to fall asleep had just gone out the window. She was too worked up to even try. Even worse was the fact that Axel didn't even seem to feel sorry about what he'd said. It might have been different if he'd taken it back immediately, or at least tried to apologize. She might not have gone off on him so badly. Still, she couldn't believe he had the nerve to say that she liked him! On the contrary, right now she hated him. More than she'd ever hated anyone. Even if she did have some deeply hidden feelings for Axel, she'd never admit it. Not even to herself. No, she would rather die than admit she actually had feelings for anyone, let alone Axel. She was an independent woman, and she didn't need a man. She didn't want one. Not now, not ever.

Axel thought about apologizing to Destiny. He really hadn't meant what he said, it just kind of came out in the heat of the moment. But then she went and started snogging with Conner! He couldn't believe it. In all honesty, it made him a bit jealous. He'd seen the way she looked at him. He knew it was him that she really liked... wasn't it? Perhaps he had only been seeing what he wanted to see. He couldn't deny that he had feelings for her. He liked her feistiness. It set her apart from any other woman he had ever met. Not to mention the fact that she was beautiful. The way her red hair flowed in the wind... The sparkle in her emerald eyes... She was absolutely breath-taking. Not that he'd admit that to her either. He didn't think she was even listening to what he said to Conner. He figured she would just go on ranting until her throat was so sore that she couldn't talk. But one sentence from him made her go silent. Apparently the feelings were not mutual. He figured he'd give her some time and then go find her, and tell her he was sorry.

Conner was even more confused now than ever. What the heck had just happened? Destiny had just kissed him, passionately, out of the blue, and then her sister had stormed off crying. What had he done? He wasn't sure whether he should go after Meriah to comfort her, or Destiny to confront her. He definitely wasn't opposed to starting a new relationship with Destiny, but he was also worried about her sister. What had made her run off crying so suddenly? Was it something he had said? He tried to remember what they'd been talking about before Axel's outburst had interrupted them, but he just couldn't conjure up a single thought about it. All he could think about was the sweet taste of Destiny's lips on his, and how wonderful a feeling it was. He hadn't kissed a girl since... He tried to remember. Since... his first girlfriend, and they had only kissed once. It was nowhere near as steamy as what had just happened with Destiny. Even though the encounter had been brief, it was exquisite. Compared to his kiss with Destiny, his kiss with her was merely a peck on the cheek.

Axel started to walk in the direction that Destiny had gone, and Conner instinctively blocked his path. Axel still looked angry, and he didn't know what his intentions were with Destiny. Axel stopped short, surprised that Conner was standing in his way.

"Let me go." Axel grumbled, glaring intently into his friend's eyes. Conner made eye contact with Axel but did not move. Axel waited a moment, then tried to shove past his friend, but Conner put out his arms to stop him. Axel's anger was growing. "What is your problem?!" He exclaimed as Conner blocked his path once again.

Conner remained unusually calm. "Let her be."

Axel glared at Conner, then jerked away from him. He walked away, grabbed one of the discarded blankets, and laid down on the ground, silently brooding.

Conner figured that Destiny still needed time to calm down. Letting Axel go after her would just start up this whole argument again. So, after a few moments hesitation that he spent glancing down at Axel and wondering if he'd really stay put if he left, he decided to try to find Meriah and figure out why she had started acting so strangely.

Conner went out of the sanctuary in the direction that she had ran, but he didn't see her. He called her name. No answer. He looked around, wondering where she could be hiding. To his right was the hallway ending at the doors that led outside. To his left was a large desk, with a door behind it. He went around the desk and opened the door to see a bunch of office supplies, none of which he recognized, aside from the stacks of paper that sat on another, much smaller desk. The room was fairly small, and he could tell that Meriah was not in it. When he came back out, he noticed the stairs leading into the basement. It was very dark down there, and Conner didn't really want to venture into the unknown, alone, without any light. He stood at the top of the stairs and called out for Meriah again. Still there was no answer. He was worried about her, but he was also worried about her sister. Destiny was a bit of a loose cannon. There was no telling what she would do in a fit of anger. Meriah was the sensible one. Wherever she was, she'd be fine. He decided to go back through the sanctuary and try to find Destiny.

Conner had a much easier time finding Destiny then Meriah. She hadn't gone very far after she'd gone through the door at the back of the sanctuary. She sat at the end of the hallway, her arms crossed, silent tears rolling down her cheeks. What is it with women crying today? As soon as Destiny realized someone was looking at her, she wiped away the tears and stood up, pretending to be fine. Conner decided not to ask if she was ok, since that was the last thing he had said to her sister before she had stormed off. Instead, he simply held out his arms, offering her a hug. She hesitated a moment, then she fell into his arms. She tried so hard to hold back her emotions, but she broke out crying again, soaking Conner's shirt. She hid her face in his chest, holding on to a vain hope that he wouldn't notice her breakdown. She wasn't proud of it, but she couldn't help it. She wanted to be strong. She hated showing any sign of weakness. Crying was a form of weakness. She never wanted anyone to see her cry. Until now, her sister had been the only one to ever see her cry.

Neither Destiny nor Conner knew how long they stood there like that. After a while, Destiny was so tired she almost fell asleep standing up. Conner picked her up in both his arms and carried her back to the sanctuary. Normally she'd never allow this, because she would insist that she was perfectly capable of walking by herself. At the moment, however, she was too worn out to care. She was so comfortable in his arms that she actually did doze off.

When Conner opened the door, he realized that Meriah had returned and was sleeping on the floor on the far side of the sanctuary. She was cuddled up with the second blanket, not leaving any for Destiny or Conner. No matter. Conner wasn't cold. He sat down against the wall, still cradling Destiny, and let her sleep peacefully in his arms.

Chapter Nine

Axel was running. From what, he didn't know. The world was dark. A faint light ahead of him gave him just enough light to see where he was going. He was in a long hallway. It seemed the longer he ran, the farther away the light became. He pushed harder, flying down the corridor as quick as he could. It seemed as though it would never end. Why was he running? What was chasing him? He never saw it, but somehow he knew that it was bad.

Finally, the long corridor opened into a large room. Axel looked up to see that the ceiling was made of glass. It was stained glass in a seemingly random pattern, but beautiful none the less. For a fleeting moment he forgot his fear. Then he looked back towards the dark hallway. It seemed to shrink down into nothing only a few yards in. He heard something that sounded like a growl, and then a scream. It came from somewhere inside the darkness. He ran back towards the deep, inky, passageway, following the sounds of the screams. It was a woman's voice. Somewhere, someone was being tortured.

He seemed to be stuck in a maze. A small amount of light came from somewhere, but he could not find its source. He turned several times, running down countless tunnels leading to somewhere unknown. His only thoughts were to help the person in pain.

Suddenly there was another voice. A man's voice. Axel recognized it immediately. It was Conner. He turned, and saw his best friend laying on the ground at the far end of the path, broken and beaten, crying out in pain. He started to run to him when he heard the woman scream again. He stopped and turned again. At the opposite end of the pathway was another body. He hadn't been able to distinguish her voice at first because he hadn't known her that long. He felt like an idiot for not realizing it sooner. It was Destiny. She didn't look any better off than Conner.

Axel didn't know what to do. Who should he run to? What could he do to help once he got there? He didn't know how to heal; that was Destiny's job. As he stood there, close to panic mode, a bright light filled the room. He had to shield his eyes from its illuminated brilliance. When the light died down, Axel found himself in a large room. High above him on a platform stood a giant throne. The chair must have been at least a hundred feet tall. On this enormous piece of work sat an even larger version of the evil king that had sent them all here. This guy could eat Axel as easily as if he were a grape. That wasn't even the worst part. In a circle around him on the floor were all the people he cared about. He saw Conner, Destiny, his mother, his brothers Jarron and Westley, his sisters Sarah and Krystal, and even his annoying little half-brother Zach. Farther out into the room he saw other people he knew, including Meriah, Rebecca, his cousins Megan and Morgan (they were twins. He still had trouble telling them apart), his uncle Bryam, his aunt Clara, and his step-father, Charles. There were many more people, it seemed everyone he had ever met in his entire lifetime was spread out on the floor around him. Even the nice pastor who let them stay in the church was there, along with his daughter. They were all crying out in pain. Every face was just as gruesome-looking as the last.

The sound of so many people groaning and crying at once was unbearable. Slowly, they all seemed to notice Axel. Every head turned to face him. Everywhere he looked there were dead eyes staring blankly back at him.

Conner was the first one to speak an intelligible word. He locked eyes with Axel and croaked, "Why?"

That is when the colossal king started to laugh. Axel looked up at him, his eyes wide with the horror of all the blood and gore around him. "Yes, Axel, why?" The dark king taunted. "This is all your fault. They are all dying because of you." He continued to laugh evilly as more and more of the wounded started to echo Conner's question.

"Why?"

"Why?"

"Why?"

The word came from anywhere and everywhere at once. Axel spun in circles, looking at all the faces of the people he once knew. Slowly, the circle of people started to close in on him as the wounded dragged themselves to their feet and made their way towards Axel.

"Why?" They demanded to know.

Conner was the closest to Axel. His face was black and blue, as well as the rest of his body. He was so bloody and bruised that he was barely recognizable. "Why?" He asked again, his nose just inches away from Axel's. Blood trickled out of his mouth when he spoke, and then suddenly he just collapsed. Conner's body lay dead at Axel's feet. Axel gasped, and knelt down beside his friend, tears coming to his eyes as his heart died with him. He tried to wake him, wishing desperately that he could help him, but it was no use.

The sound of the evil king's laughter echoed through Axel's head, endlessly taunting him.

Destiny was next. She stumbled right up into Axel's face, demanded that he answer their simple question, and then dropped dead at his feet. Slowly, everyone arose like zombies and stumbled their way over to Axel, only to be left without an answer as they fell on the floor dead. Axel was soon surrounded by a hundred corpses. The king continued to laugh.

Axel wanted to answer them, but he couldn't. He just didn't know. He didn't know why, and he probably never would.

Suddenly, Dante Sinclaire appeared next to Axel. He had both of his swords drawn. He raised them, ready to sever Axel and add one more cadaver to the graveyard.

Axel looked around desperately. There was nowhere to go. He was surrounded by dead people. He let out a scream as Dante came in for the kill.

Axel sat bolt upright on the ground, breathing heavily. Highly disoriented, he looked around trying to figure out where he was. Was he dead? Is this what happened when you died? He couldn't remember actually being killed, but then again, he couldn't remember much of anything right now.

"Whaaat?" Destiny groaned groggily, woken by his scream. She nuzzled her head into Conner's chest, ready to fall back asleep.

Hearing her voice sent Axel into a frenzy. It all came rushing back. The king. The people. Death. So much death.

Next thing Destiny knew, Axel was pulling her away from Conner to face him. "You're alright!" He exclaimed, throwing his arms around her in a giant bear hug. It was a wonder that he didn't wake up Conner with how loud he was being, or how roughly he pulled Destiny away from him. Axel didn't care if he woke up the whole neighborhood. He was just happy that everything was okay. He was back at the church. It was all just one big horrible dream.

Destiny glared at him, angry that he'd woken her from such a deep and restful sleep for no apparent reason. "Of course I am alright." *You bothersome imbecile!* She added in her head. She was tired. She had been quite comfortable.

She wanted to go back to Conner and go back to sleep. "What is the matter with you?" She asked, clearly annoyed.

"I... I had this terrible nightmare..." The look of terror on Axel's face concerned Destiny. She tried to focus on what he was saying. He told her all about the mammoth king and the tortured people. He told her how he'd seen her die at his feet.

Destiny was only a little shaken by his words. She was too tired to fully grasp the gravity of the situation. "It was only a dream." She said, putting her hand on his shoulder. "Do not worry. We are all fine, see?" She gestured around the church to where the others were still sleeping. With that, she turned back towards Conner, ready to drift off into unconsciousness again in his arms.

Axel grabbed her arm to stop her. "Let us wake the others."

"What?!" Destiny cried out. That was the *last* thing she wanted to hear. Not only had she been so rudely awakened in the middle of the night, now he expected her to *stay* awake and wake up everyone else? For what? To tell them of his dream? They could hear it later. In the morning. After they'd gotten a full night's sleep. "It is still late. Please, let us sleep."

"If we are going to win this battle, we need to find a way to get stronger, a way to practice our skills as much and as soon as possible. I will wake Conner." Axel said, clearly jealous of the way Destiny was clinging to his best friend.

"Why can it not wait until the morning?" Destiny asked, not getting out of Axel's way. She still planned on going back to cuddling with Conner.

Which is exactly why Axel didn't want to let her go. He'd rather they all got up now to start their day early, and get as much done as possible.

Destiny clearly wasn't a morning person, and she was just about as stubborn as a mule. Instead of arguing, she walked back over to Conner, sat down on gingerly on his lap, and laid her head on his shoulder. He moaned once, and Destiny was scared she had woken him. If Conner opened his eyes, there would be no denying Axel getting everyone else up to start on whatever it was he had planned for the day. Thankfully, Conner just repositioned his legs and then put an arm around Destiny and went right back to sleep. She grinned and eventually nodded off.

Meriah was the first to wake up in the morning. That is, aside from Axel who had never gone back to sleep. She sat up, yawning as she stretched and looked around. The first thing to catch her eye was her sister snuggled up so nice and cozy with Conner. The sight made her angry. Didn't anyone notice her? Didn't anyone care how she felt? Of course, she couldn't really blame them, she hadn't told either of them how she cared for Conner, but still. Her sister at least should notice how she looks at him. How she longs to be with him. Sisters are supposed to be in tune with each other's feelings. Destiny had known her her whole life. She should notice when there was something different about her.

Perhaps her shyness would be her own undoing. She needed to be bold and brave and put herself out there if she wanted to be noticed. Isn't that what her sister was always saying? But what if the person she liked didn't return her feelings? She would only get hurt, and then things between them would be awkward. She glanced over at her sister again. Maybe it was a good thing that she hadn't mentioned to Conner how much she liked him. It seemed pretty obvious that he liked her sister much more than her anyway. Her anger gave way to tears as she started to cry.

"Are you alright?" A voice asked cautiously behind her.

Meriah jumped and quickly wiped away her tears. She had thought she was the only one awake. "I am just fine." She lied.

Axel stood there awkwardly, not knowing what to do or say. He wasn't sure how to make a girl feel better. He knew she was probably lying about being okay, but he didn't want to upset her any more so decided not to press the issue.

Axel turned instead and walked over to where Conner and Destiny were both still sleeping peacefully. "Time to get up." He said loudly. Destiny groaned and moved a bit, but did not get up. Axel walked closer, leaned down, and roughly shook them both awake. Destiny jumped and fell backwards. Luckily, Axel caught her before her head hit the floor. Her head in his hands, Axel grinned down at her and said, "Good morning."

Destiny glared up at him, still not happy to be woken up so harshly.

Once Conner was fully awake, he immediately started to mess with his hair. Destiny laughed.

Apparently during the night the rope that held up Destiny's dress had become loose. When she got up to stretch, her dress didn't come with her. She screamed in embarrassed horror, grabbing it and running for one of the back rooms. Her sister ran after her. Of the two of them, Meriah was the one who knew how to sew and cook and do all of the things that a good housewife should know how to do. After a little searching, Meriah found a needle and thread and set to work on fixing her sister's dress for her. It was still pretty tattered-looking, but at least it stayed up on its own. A few hours later, Destiny returned to the sanctuary carrying the rope that had once belonged to Axel. She returned this to him, and then asked what his big plan for the day was.

Before he had a chance to answer, they were all startled by someone else entering the room. "Good morning!" Pastor Chad said cheerily, looking around at all their stunned faces. They had all forgotten he was there. "Traveling through time again today? Or do you plan on battling the medieval king again?" He laughed. He was the only one who thought it was funny. He decided to change the subject. "Are you guys hungry? I went out early this morning and bought some breakfast foods."

He led them back out into the main hall and to the set of stairs leading into the basement. It looked pretty dark down there. Axel and his friends were hesitant to follow. At the bottom of the steps, however, Chad touched something on the wall and the whole bottom floor sprang to life. At least that's what it looked like to the rest of them. Chad knew it was simply a light switch. Axel, Conner, Destiny, and Meriah thought it was magic. Chad had a table set up in the middle of the basement floor with a variety of different things to eat. Most likely he had set this up while Meriah and her sister were busy fixing Destiny's dress. It had taken up most of the morning.

On the table sat a few wondrous items that no one but Chad had ever seen before. There was a box labeled "Cheerios", a yellow jug that claimed it held milk, and a stack of some odd-looking things that had a grid pattern on them. Chad called them "wah-fulls". Axel had never seen a wah-full before. He wondered what a wah would look like if it was empty. Perhaps he just meant that right now the plate is full of wahs. He decided not to think about it too much. He was starved and couldn't wait to taste all the strange new food. Axel filled his plate with eggs, bacon, and two of the mysterious wah-fulls.

During their meal, Chad's daughter showed up to join them. "Jacquelynn," Her father said sternly, "What are you doing here? You're supposed to be in school."

Jack sighed. "I was, dad. I'm at lunch. I'll be back in class by one. Promise."

Chad checked his watch. It was already 12:23. "Jackie," he said impatiently, "You know it takes twenty minutes to walk to your school from here. You don't have enough time to-"

"I'll be there in five if you'll give me a ride." Jack interrupted, stuffing her smiling mouth full of waffles.

"I really don't feel comfortable leaving..."

"Oh, do not worry about us." Axel cut in, "We will be gone as soon as we finish eating. I would like to thank you again for letting us stay."

Jack grinned. "There, see? Problem solved." She really didn't want to go back to school. She wanted to stay here and hear more about the adventures of the four cryptic people who had magically shown up in front of the church. However, she knew that her father would never allow her to skip school, so she had to learn as much as she could in the short time that they had together.

Jack never made it back to school.

After everyone was finished eating, Jack followed them outside to say goodbye. They all made sure to thank Chad again before leaving.

"You're welcome. May the Lord be with you." Chad said. Then he turned and walked towards his office, looking for his car keys.

"What is the Lord?" Conner asked. Axel shoved him outside before he could ask any more stupid questions.

"Ok, guys, so what's the plan?" Asked Jack, the moment her dad was out of ear-shot. Axel and Conner looked at each other. They didn't really have a plan. They were just going to go practice hunting in the woods or something. They were pretty much making this all up as they went along. Maybe they'd even ask Destiny to teach them a little magic. How hard could it be?

It was actually Meriah who spoke first. "I think we should find Dante. Dante will lead us to the king. We want answers, and Dante is the only one who has them."

"That is a good idea," said Conner approvingly, but then, looking around, added, "But how are we supposed to find him? This place is huge! He could be anywhere."

Jack wanted to know more about Dante, like what he looked like, and what they were going to do when they found him. She wasn't going to have to wait long.

"Dante seems to have a knack for just popping up whenever he is needed, so I have a feeling he will find us." said Destiny.

As if on cue, Dante was suddenly there, standing right in front of Destiny. She scowled at him. "Did someone call me?" He asked, a smug smile on his face.

"Speak of the devil." said Meriah, who was standing right next to her sister, hands on her hips, wearing a similar look of distaste.

Dante turned and grinned at her. "I'm flattered, really. But we're not related."

Jack stared wide-eyed at the new comer. He had long blonde hair and extremely dark eyes. He was about the same height as Conner, but was much more built. He wore a long black jacket that almost brushed the ground when he walked. His chest was bare, revealing his sexy six-pack. Jack noticed his chest was smooth and devoid of hair. His pants seemed to be made from the same simple material as Axel's and Conner's, and they were also black. A girl had appeared with him. She was much younger than him, looking to be about ten years old.

"You're Dante?" Jack asked in awe. She'd never seen a gorgeous guy appear out of thin air before. She'd never seen anyone appear out of thin air before. She was dumbfounded.

Dante chuckled. He looked her up and down, then seemed to approve. "Who are you?"

"Jaquelynn!" The voice made everyone jump. Everyone but Dante. He turned casually to face whoever had appeared behind them. It was Pastor Chad. "We're going to be late! Hurry, get in the car!" He stopped momentarily to look at Dante and the little girl.

Dante, not interested in Chad in the least, took advantage of this interruption and lashed out at Conner with one of his swords. His sword was massive, easily three times larger than Axel's. Yet, Dante was quite capable of lifting his blade and swinging it with ease, despite its overwhelming mass.

Conner was not prepared, and nowhere near ready. He had thought maybe they could talk this out. Figure out what had gone wrong, and what was up with the big scary king guy.

Conner was wrong.

As Dante's sword flew towards the unsuspecting Conner, Chad was the only one to notice. Since everyone else had turned to look at him, he was now the only one still looking at Dante. "Look out!" He screamed, throwing his arm out and pointing his finger at Dante.

A second later, Conner would have died. Dante's sword sliced through the air where Conner's head had just been. Conner ducked out of the way with not a moment to spare. Conner did a barrel roll to get farther away, quickly regained his footing, and then got his bow ready and took aim.

Dante was just too quick. If Conner was going to have a chance in this fight he was going to need a sword. Or someone with a sword to fight for him.

Axel pulled out his sword and charged at Dante, who easily disappeared right as he was about to impale him. Dante, now way out of Axel's reach, laughed as the force of Axel's swipe sent him stumbling over his own feet and landing with his face in the dirt.

Dante's next attack on Conner didn't miss. As Dante appeared closer to Conner, he wasted no time before charging him again. Conner, quickly re-aiming his bow, shot an arrow just as Dante's sword came flying towards him. The arrow hit Dante's arm, just below his shoulder, throwing off his aim. Even though it wasn't the life-ending blow that Dante had intended, Conner was still hurt pretty badly. Dante didn't seem bothered by the arrow. He left it there, sticking out of his arm, as if he hadn't even noticed it piercing his flesh.

Instead of slicing through Conner's skull, Dante's blade sliced his arm. Conner screamed in agony as the sword went down to his bone. Thankfully, that's as far as it went. Still, the cut was very deep, and gushing blood. His left arm now completely useless, Conner put his bow back over his shoulder and ran. For what, he didn't know. He was finished.

Dante could appear and re-appear at will. He was strong, while Conner was growing weaker by the minute. What was left to do? As a last desperate attempt, Conner tried reasoning. "Why, Dante?" Conner cried out between labored breaths as he ran, "Why did you succumb to him?"

Axel, having recovered from his embarrassing tumble, was more determined than ever to kill Dante. He didn't think about the fact that he had never before taken a life. It didn't occur to him that this was a person who still had friends who cared for him. He forgot that he was the only one who knew where the king was, and that could explain any of this. All he could see was a monster. A terrible being that was trying to murder his best friend. For no reason. He stood up in time to see Dante's unrealistically large sword swipe Conner's arm. Conner's howl fueled Axel's hatred even more, like a greedy fire it consumed him, his every thought, every movement. As Conner started to
run, so did Axel. Axel raised his sword high above his head with both his hands, and let out a deep, thundering roar as he charged full force at Dante.

Axel's resounding bellow is what saved Dante's life. Hearing the vociferous wail, he turned, and whipped his sword around mere seconds before Axel's blade would have sliced his brain in half. Dante held his sword in both his hands, holding back his enemy's sword. This, however, was not done as easily as the rest of the battle. For the first time since they met, Axel sensed a change in Dante. His cocky demeanor had broken, if only for a moment, and Axel registered fear in his eyes.

That was when Conner asked his question: "Why?" Conner was still running, or trying to. He was weak. He had his back turned to Dante. The world was starting to turn dark. He had lost so much blood. Too much blood. He didn't hear the clang of swords. He didn't know Axel was fighting for him. His words came out as a mumble, probably not even noticed by anyone else around. At long last, Conner gave up, falling to the ground. "Why?" He cried out miserably, using the last of his breath. He thought he felt soft hands caressing his wounds, accompanied by a sweet voice. The angels had come to take him away. He was ready. Ready for the pain to end. The pain slowly melted away as Conner slipped into unconsciousness.

Axel heard Conner's cry and it brought him back to his dream, making him lose focus for a moment and allowing Dante to break out of the bind. "He gives me my power!" Dante yelled, though Conner was no longer listening. Something had changed again in Dante. He was now perfectly content with battling Axel rather than Conner. His fury seemed matched with Axel's as they fought it out.

Pastor Chad watched the scene with wide eyes. He was frozen to the spot. His brain seemed to have shut off. He had no idea what was going on, and there was nothing he could do about it. So he just stood there, mouth agape, watching the whole scene unfold. It was like he was watching a movie. He gasped and yelled, but it didn't feel real to him. None of this felt real to him. If he had been thinking clearly, he would have gotten out his cell phone and called the police. He would have grabbed Jaquelynn and kept her safe. Still, his mind was in overload, and he just stood there, rooted to the spot, stunned and helpless.

The girls were not far off. However, the first sight of blood kicked Destiny's brain into high gear. Both Destiny and Meriah were jolted back into reality and ran to try to help Conner.

There was another girl there too, but everyone had quite forgotten about her. She had a round, childish face, with bright brown eyes and auburn hair that fell just past her shoulders. Her name was Katara and she had been watching everything Dante did with great interest. When he was shot, she gasped, and ran closer to see if she could help him. Looking up at her friend, half in fear, and half in question of what to do, she saw in his eyes that it was time. She seemed unsure at first, but then with an encouraging nod from Dante barely noticeable to anyone else, she turned on the girls, her eyes growing dark as she let the powers of darkness take over her. She smiled as flames engulfed her hands. Meriah immediately transformed and flew up high where the girl couldn't reach her. Destiny sighed. *Classic Meriah. Flying away rather than facing the problem.*

Jack had been watching the scene pretty much the same way as her father. Her survival instincts took over, however, when a fireball was thrown in her direction, just barely missing her head. The intense heat burned her face as it passed, making her cry out in pain. Without thinking, she ran towards her father and shoved him back and out of the way. Surprised and unaware, Chad tumbled to the ground easily. The two of them sat on the ground, huddled together next to the church, unable to take their eyes off what was happening.

Destiny transformed and let out a deep growl. She could move much more swiftly in her tiger form, and was able to dodge the fire more effectively. However, now she was too far away and incapable of helping Conner.

"Holy crap!" Jack exclaimed. She had been similarly amazed when Meriah transformed, but she was just a big blue bird. It was cool, but really not that impressive. A tiger though! Now that was pretty freaking awesome.

Katara, not expecting this transformation, retreated, not knowing what else to do. She was still young. She was scared. She didn't want to get hurt. She just wanted to protect Dante. Like he protected her.

Destiny continued to growl threateningly, but did not pursue the girl. She transformed again, ignoring the fact that she had ruined her dress a second time, and ran to Conner. Frantically, she assessed the situation and started the healing process. Meriah circled in the sky above her, keeping an eye on Katara. The central battle between Axel and Dante continued to clash noisily in the background as Destiny tried to concentrate on her work. It wasn't long before Conner was fully healed. He had fainted from the loss of so much blood, but Destiny had been able to reach him before his light had fully gone out. He would be unconscious for a while, but he would be ok.

Meriah swooped down and grabbed the biggest piece of her sister's shredded dress in her claws, helping her to hide her nakedness. Thanking her sister, Destiny stood and took the material, wrapping it around herself like a towel. Then she went over to Meriah's discarded dress and helped her into it as quickly as possible. Then, together they managed to pick up Conner and haul him towards the church.

Chad saw them coming and at long last his brain began to function. He jumped up, opened the door, and escorted the three of them inside. There was no longer any doubt in Chad's mind that they were telling the truth. Jack had been right to trust them, and he felt ashamed for having been so harsh with them yesterday. He vowed to himself that as soon as he got the chance he would apologize, and do whatever he could to help them.

Chapter Ten

Rebecca had finished telling her story, and neither Jarron or Sairynn knew what to say. They were two feet away from a vampire! A real live vampire. A demon creature that lived by sucking the life out of others. Who knew such creatures even really existed? Jarron would have laughed at the very thought of it earlier that same day, but now here he was, face-to-face with one of nature's most terrifying creations. Should they try to run? Would it even do them any good? *Get a hold of yourself, Jarron.* He scolded himself, *Vampires are dangerous, of course, but this is Rebecca we are talking about.* He paused, studying the beautiful woman in front of him. *It's no wonder she never returned home. She was worried she might hurt someone she loved. Or worse, what if her family didn't accept her the way she was now? Learning that your daughter is missing is one thing, but finding out that she has been transformed into a blood thirsty beast is something else entirely.* He almost felt bad for her as he thought, *How lonely she must have been!* Then he looked over at Vincent. *The incredible strength, the fast, precise movements, it all makes sense now.*

Jarron and Sairynn were sitting in the grass, chit-chatting with two vampires as casually as if they were merely talking about the weather. *Vampires.* Jarron shuddered. The word alone gave him nightmares. Rebecca he trusted, but he knew nothing of this man. He could just be waiting for the right moment to pounce. As if he knew Jarron was thinking about him, Vincent turned his head to look at him. Jarron immediately looked away. Those glowing orange eyes really creeped him out.

"It wasn't too long after that that I met Vincent." Rebecca was saying. Jarron turned his attention back to her. Her eyes seemed calmer, kinder, and... not the same color that he thought they were. He could have sworn she had light blue eyes before, but now they were a much darker green color. Jarron pondered over this for a few moments, wondering exactly what it was that caused her eyes to change. Rebecca, oblivious to the fact that Jarron was not listening to a word she said as he focused on the strangeness of the color of her iris's, smiled over at Vincent, who sat on the ground a few feet away facing her. Her perfectly clear memory took her back to the moments before she first saw his face...

The smell of so much fresh blood is what first attracted her to the scene. She ran through the woods, her adrenaline pumping more excessively the faster she ran. With each step, her hunger grew. This was going to be a magnificent feast. Anticipation made her mouth water as she followed the delicious aroma on what seemed like an endless journey to find its source.

When she got to the edge of the woods, she finally found the origin of the fragrance: a man was being attacked. He had already been stabbed twice, and delicious red liquid was oozing out of his body. Her throat burned with thirst. She had not consumed anything for three days. The urge to attack was almost unbearable. It took all of her willpower to hold back until the battle was done. She did not want to lose control and kill everybody. *If the attacked one is already dying,* she reasoned within herself, *what is the harm in taking his blood? He isn't going to be needing it anymore.* At last, the bloody feast was left alone to die. Almost instantly she was hovering over top of the freshly prepared meal...

"However, I was not dead." Vincent cut in, "My powers had been lost. My arms were no longer attached to my body, and there was more blood on the ground around me than there was left in my body. Still somehow, I managed to cling to life for just a little while longer. The pain was unimaginable."

Jarron tried (unsuccessfully) not to picture the scene. The sight of blood made him woozy. He looked over at Sairynn, who looked about as bad as he felt.

Sairynn was white as a ghost and shaking uncontrollably. He wanted to run, but couldn't. He was frozen to the spot. He started to hyperventilate, and before long, he passed out.

Jarron felt bad for him, and wanted to see if he was alright, but was afraid to move. With a vampire on either side of you, there was not much you could do.

"Somewhere deep inside of me, there was a part of my heart that still cared." Rebecca said, ignoring the interruption and stepping back into the memories of her past.

Rebecca looked down into the eyes of the fallen man. They were only slightly open, and it was obvious that he was very weak and they would soon close for the very last time. She didn't know this man, but still she felt bad for him. She remembered the pain of the day she was attacked and changed into a monster. She knew how it felt to be inches away from death. The compassion that filled her soul was not quite enough to stop her from becoming intoxicated on all of the blood that lay around and on him, but it did stop her from finishing him off.

After she had taken her fill of his blood, she pushed his arms back into place and then released the poison from her fangs into his blood stream. His heart was very weak, but the venom worked very fast. She bit into his chest, introducing the toxin directly to his heart. She figured this would be the quickest way to save him, if that was still possible. She watched as his heart turned black and stopped beating, and for a moment she thought she had lost him. However, the cancer continued to spread. The blackened heart began beating again, pumping the poison through his veins where his blood used to be. Slowly, he regained consciousness. He tried to get up, but she forced him back down. The process was not yet complete. As she had hoped, the transformation also began to heal his wounds. The giant hole in his chest shrank down to nothing, and his arms were reattached to his body. In just minutes he was good as new. Aside from the ripped clothes, dried blood, and the fact that he was now a blood-thirsty monster.

Vincent got to his feet, staring at his arms and chest in wide-eyed wonder. He was amazed, confused, grateful, more than a little scared, but most of all thirsty. He was suddenly overcome with the desire to drink something. He thought to himself that he was dehydrated, delirious, and probably still within inches of death. This miraculous recovery was merely an illusion. A final hallucination before drifting off into a never-ending sleep.

It was bright. Much too bright. He shielded his eyes from the glaring sun. He swore a few minutes ago that it had been a cool Autumn day, but now it felt as if it was the middle of summer at high noon in the Lut Desert in Iran. Is this what Hell felt like? Is that where he was going? Perhaps he was already dead and he was now just a ghost, doomed to wander the earth for all of eternity.

Vincent looked around as his eyes adjusted to the brightness of the world around him, and noticed there was a woman standing beside him. She had very beautiful green eyes, and long, reddish-brown hair that danced up and down in ringlets around her face. She would have been gorgeous if not for the fact that she was covered in almost as much dried blood as he was. Especially around her mouth. That last part really freaked him out.

"Who are you?" He squeaked. His voice was hoarse from the overwhelming thirst he was experiencing. He instinctively placed a hand on it to try to soothe it. He wondered briefly if she was the devil, and she'd come to drag him away. *But isn't Satan supposed to be a man?*

She smiled, revealing the inside of her mouth to be just as bloody as the outside. Vincent cringed. She ran her tongue across her teeth, wiping off some of the blood and tasting it. It creeped Vincent out even more. He looked away. He felt like he was going to be sick.

Jarron had the same sick feeling in his stomach. He was seconds away from doubling over and spiting vomit all over these monsters. He tried his best to remain strong as he reluctantly listened to the rest of the story.

Rebecca grinned even wider, knowing that she had successfully succeeded in saving his life. Now she wouldn't have to be so alone. She would have a friend who would live forever, just like her. She would have to help him, of course; teach him about his new abilities and how to hunt for animals. Finally, she would have a purpose again. Something to live for. Her smile grew as she became more excited about the future they were going to spend together.

That's when he noticed it. Or, to be more accurate, *them*. This girl had fangs. Suddenly it all made sense. He was standing next to a real-life blood-sucking vampire. So she wasn't Lucifer come to take him away at all, but, really, which was worse? Just this morning he had thought that vampires and demons and all that was just the stuff of myths and legends. They weren't real, just stories made up to scare you into being a good person. Now he realized that he couldn't have been more wrong. For if vampires were real, what wasn't? Could there really be satanic demons such as these roaming the earth? Are there real witches? And Werewolves? At the moment he believed that anything was possible.

Sudden movement to his left reminded him that he was not alone. He turned his head towards the mysterious woman. No, scratch that. Towards the monster. He was scared. He thought about running, but he didn't know where to go. Vampires were fast. Unbelievably fast. There was nothing he could do. He was trapped. And thirsty. Unbelievably thirsty. He hoped she'd just kill him quickly before he died of thirst.

His adrenaline spiked immediately. There was a murderous beast a few feet away from him, seductively licking blood off her teeth, and smiling at him like this was some kind of game. Blood. *His* blood. It wasn't until just then that the full gravity of the situation came down upon Vincent. He now knew why he was dying of thirst. The thought of what he had to do to quench it was unbearable.

The truth hit him hard like a critical blow to the chest, knocking the wind out of him. Or at least it would have if he had been breathing. He realized then that he hadn't actually taken a breath since he saw the woman. But his lungs didn't hurt. He no longer needed to breathe. It was the strangest sensation, to be standing there, seemingly alive, and yet not breathing. He could breathe (he took a deep breath just to be sure) but the attempt now seemed futile. What was the point?

"If I was going to kill you, you would be dead already." She smiled. It was a friendly smile, although it was also a little mischievous. "You should be thanking me. I just saved your life." She winked at him. *Why not have a little fun with him?* She thought, eyeing him cautiously to see what he would do. She needed to teach him how to run and hunt and quench that terrible thirst that she knew was building up inside of him. The first few days are the worst, and the least she could do was to try to make it a little more fun for him.

Vincent's eyes flashed red with anger as he glared at the woman a few feet away from him. "What have you done to me?" He growled.

She backed away ever-so-slightly. She thought she was doing the right thing by saving his life. Maybe she had made a mistake. Her brain worked fast. This was going to be slightly harder than she thought. *That's ok, I like a challenge.* She had a plan. She ran.

Thinking she was running away scared, Vincent followed her. He was fast. Inhumanly fast. He stumbled over his own feet and hit the ground. Hard. He heard the woman's voice teasing him to come and get her. His anger took over again as he tried to run after her again, a bit more cautiously this time. He got used to his new speed quickly and followed the sound of her voice. Everything around him was so much clearer now. He could hear the insects as they flew by, smell the grass beneath his feet, and see the trees growing around him. Following this woman would be too easy. Every step she took he could hear, every time she spoke, every bit of earth that crunched under her weight. Her swift movements sent her uncommon yet exquisite scent back towards him. She led him deep into the woods, on a long and twisting path. A human would have been lost almost immediately, but he managed to stay fairly close to her as she bounded over and under branches, expertly making her way to the heart of the forest.

Suddenly he stopped short when a wonderful new aroma met his nose. It was different from the girl's, and filled him with an unheard of hunger. He began following this new scent, no longer able to find her smell. He didn't care. This new aroma overpowered everything else and he was drove forward with an urgency to find its source. He came to a small clearing. He had found the woman. At her feet was a freshly killed deer. She motioned for him to come closer.

"It is not the best, but it is satisfying." She said simply.

Vincent growled at her. He fought to keep his self-control. "Not as good as mine, huh?" He said sarcastically. He tried to resist, but the pain in his throat urged him to attack. Reluctantly he gave in to his hunger, and took a bite of the deer. Well, he intended to just take a bite out of it. Once the fresh meat touched his lips, instinct took over. He drained most of the blood out of the poor creature before he was filled.

"Not one of my finest moments." Vincent said, seemingly embarrassed. "But that is just who I am now. I am not proud of it, but it cannot be helped." He combed his fingers through his long black hair, pushing it back out of his eyes. "After I got over my anger, Rebecca introduced herself properly and we became friends." He smiled at her as if they were more than just friends. Jarron shuddered again.

"Our happiness was short lived, however." Rebecca said, sadly, "Shortly thereafter I was whisked away to this castle, where I've been imprisoned ever since. It was strange, one moment I was walking, talking, and laughing with Vincent, and the next second I was behind bars. I don't know what magic The Wizard used to keep me here, but no matter how hard I tried, I could not break free."

"It was a mystery to me also, but I knew it had to be The Wizard's doing. Finally getting back at me for abandoning him, I suppose. Who wants to work for a coward who never shows their face, anyway?" Vincent glared at the ruined castle as he spoke, as if The Wizard were still there, listening.

"You abandoned The Wizard?" Rebecca asked, genuinely interested.

"In a way, yes. I used to be his messenger boy, running around and doing all his dirty work. All when I was very young. My earliest memories are of his voice telling me where to go and what to do. I still never saw his face. So, anyways, a while back, I think I was only about seven years old, The Wizard gave me my first big task. He handed me this small crystal and told me that it contained a great many powers. I was to take this crystal to the royal family where they would have a grand ceremony and give this power to their newborn baby son. On my way to the castle, I saw a man stealing food from a nearby merchant, and I recognized him as the same thief that was wanted for attempting to steal jewels from the royal family. I thought to myself, 'The Wizard will be so proud of me when I bring him the wanted thief.' So I got out the crystal and tried to summon its powers to use against the thief. But instead of hurting him, the stone gave to the thief the mighty Power of the Dragons that was supposed to go to the new prince! Knowing I could not return to The Wizard after messing up so badly, I went up to the thief and vowed my services to him, secretly praying for a way to one day fix what I had done. The thief, however, was a master pick-pocket, and soon had my crystal for himself. Using the various powers that the crystal gave to him (and some he gave to me), the thief took over the royal kingdom and sat himself down on the throne as the king of this land. Now, the thief (whose name is Sepheroth) had a wife who was great with child. Everything he stole had been to try to get better care for her. Now that he was living as a king, she had everything she needed. But the new powers that Sepheroth had acquired had changed him. He was now a much darker person, and she did not love him anymore. Overcome with stress, the new queen went into labor early."

Rebecca gasped and stared at Vincent with wide eyes. "Did she lose the baby?"

"Yes and no." Vincent answered cryptically. "She had the baby, but she died during the birthing process. The baby was small, but healthy. Sepheroth, however, blamed the child for his wife's death and abandoned it outside in the woods, leaving it to die. More recently, the king heard a rumor that the child had somehow survived. He sent a spy out into the land to try to figure out the location of the child, cursing himself for not killing the baby when it was born. He vowed to kill the boy before he realized his true powers and took over his kingdom. His spy, however, got sent back to him with very little information on the whereabouts of his son. It was this same spy that tried to kill me. On Sepheroth's orders. After all I had done for him! But, as you know, Becca found me, and now, here I am." He smiled over at Rebecca, then turned away, his face growing dark. "One day soon," He said, the malice in his voice growing with every word, "I plan to find Sepheroth and make him pay for what he has done."

"Vincent." Rebecca scolded, as if she were talking to a naughty child. "I did not save your life so that you could run back there and get yourself killed."

"Then why did you save me?" He turned on her, his eyes glowing red with anger. She gasped slightly at the intensity of his glare, and her green eyes flickered to light blue once more. He waited for her to reply, locking his terrifying stare on her face. She didn't respond. Instead, she cast her eyes downward looking beaten.

"Hold on, back up." Jarron spoke up suddenly. Rebecca and Vincent had both forgotten he was there. "You said that the baby was left in the woods? How long ago was this?"

"I don't know, about 18 years, why?" Vincent's anger was instantly replaced by confusion.

Jarron grinned at the bewildered looks of both Rebecca and Vincent. "I think I might know who Sepheroth's son is."

Chapter Eleven

Axel's face glistened with sweat from the hot summer heat as he clashed swords with the mysterious Dante. He wondered for a moment how Dante could stand to wear such a long, heavy, black jacket outside in this weather. Even without a shirt on underneath, he had to be dying in all that thick, dark material. Axel was getting tired of fighting. *Clang! Clang! Clang!* The sound echoed around his brain, never ending. Dante was so quick with his sword that Axel could never get in any offensive moves, and was forced to only block and parry with him. Dante seemed to be very amused by this. He laughed and moved around swiftly and easily as if he were playing a child's game. Axel was too tired to be angry. He was slowing down. If something didn't happen soon, he'd be done for.

Quite suddenly, there was a great burst of wind that filled the air around them, distracting everyone, even Dante. Dante looked up, hearing words that no one else could hear: *Dante, Katara, retreat!* Then, just as suddenly, the air became still again.

Axel spun around, looking to the sky and all around for the source of the sudden gust of air but saw no one, or no thing. Dante took one final stab at Axel, catching him in his gut, before breaking away from the fight and running to Katara. As soon as he grabbed her hand, they vanished.

Axel ignored the searing pain in his belly. He knew this was not over yet. As everyone else ran into the church, Axel remained, waiting. For what, he wasn't really sure. His senses were on high alert, watching for the slightest sign of movement. Another attack of some kind. Anything. Perhaps Dante had gone for backup. Or he was merely playing with him. Axel was but a mere mouse caught in the sly cat's trap. The sudden disappearance of Dante seemed to give him a second wind, but how long could he last? Just then, he heard movement next to the church, and turned, readying his sword for attack. He slowly started to walk that way when he heard something else.

It was the same voice that Dante had heard in the wind, but now it was much louder and speaking to Axel. "You are pathetic."

Axel spun back around, looking for the source of the voice. He seemed to still be alone. "Who is there?" he yelled out to the empty space before him.

"It is I, Sepheroth." Replied the deep and growling voice, "Your father."

"What!?" Axel shouted, lowering his sword in stunned confusion. He was ready for a fight, a confrontation, something, anything but this. His father?! That was the very last thing he had expected to hear today. Why would this disembodied voice pretend to be his father? Didn't he know that his father's name was James? And that he had died a long time ago when Axel was young? Axel raised his sword once more, and yelled, "Show yourself, coward! I know you are not my father, for he died long ago, and-"

The deep voice laughed evilly as the dark king appeared in front of him.

"You!" yelled Axel, hating the king more with each passing second. "You are not my father! My father was a common peasant, a good man who worked hard for everything he got." Axel yelled, trying to hold back the tears and the pain that came rushing back at the thought of his father. "His name was James Alexander Rynne you fool!" He lashed out at the king, who easily evaded his blade.

"You know that it's true." said the king, ignoring his insult, "Take a better look at that sword you're holding. You think a common peasant would have one as magnificent as that? That sword was stolen from me many years ago, and I had given up hope that I would ever see it again. But now, here we are." He disappeared again and his voice whispered from somewhere behind Axel, "That sword was not used by your 'father' to fight. No," The king appeared in front of him again, wearing a smug smile, "that sword was used to kill him."

"NO! No, that is impossible!" His sword, his beauty! No, he wouldn't believe it. He couldn't. "My father was sickly; he didn't die by a sword!" Axel protested. He again lashed out at the king, who disappeared before the blade got anywhere close to him. Axel heard his evil laugh as he appeared behind him. He was toying with him. Axel knew he would not be able to hurt the king with his sword, but his anger drove him to keep fighting. His tired bones had a new energy, fueled by his hatred towards the king. No one insults Axel's father and lives to tell the tale. *No one.*

"Believe it or not, you can't change the truth. That sword has special powers that you cannot even begin to comprehend. When combined with the legendary power of the Black Dragon, you can inflict curses with it, without even leaving a scratch. That illness that you spoke of was actually a curse that ate up dear Jimmy boy from the inside out. Just one tiny scrape after you're affected and-" he snapped his fingers, "Bye bye daddy." He chuckled evilly, disappearing again as Axel stared at his sword, silently letting the words of the king sink into his head. "Why don't you give it to someone who knows how to use it?" The voice of the king taunted, still unseen.

Axel growled, spinning around and lashing out with his sword, but all he sliced through was air. "I know how to use my sword! Stand and fight me like a man and I will prove it to you!"

The great king appeared before him, shaking his head and laughing. "If you wish to face me you will meet me at my new castle." He paused, and then said, as an afterthought, "If you need a little inspiration, just remember this." He snapped his fingers again, and this time Destiny appeared beside him, floating in midair, gagged and tied up, struggling to break free of her bondage. Axel reached out to her, dropping his sword to the ground in the process. But before he could reach her she was gone again. Axel glared at the king, a new level of loathing growing within him. He reached down for his sword and dove at the king. The king vanished again in a round of dark chuckles, leaving Axel face-first in the dirt as his built-up momentum hit nothing. Axel experienced a vindictive malevolence like he had never felt before. As he got up, he heard the voice one last time. "Until then, farewell my son." The voice spoke right behind Axel's head, he spun to face the evil king, just in time to see him raise his hand at him, as if telling him to stop. The king's hand was a mere inches from Axel's chest as he started to release his dark magic over him. Then he disappeared for the final time, his evil laugh whispering through the wind. The sound of Axel's sword hitting the ground as he fell back into the dirt echoed around the area.

Back inside the church, everyone gasped at the sudden disappearance of Destiny. She had just helped to lay Conner down, and was trying to make him comfortable when all of a sudden she was just gone. Conner's head hit the padding on the church pew with a soft thud as her hand vanished from underneath it.

"Destiny!" Meriah cried out, not believing what she had just seen. Then a second later, she was gone too.

Jack stood staring at the empty space where her friends had just been. For the first time since she had met the strange new travelers, she realized that this was all too real. The magic, the adventure, and the danger. Would she be next? How could she protect herself? There was no way they could have seen this coming, for there was nothing to see. Two people just vanished. Where had they gone? Who had taken them? *I suppose I really shouldn't be that surprised, I saw that Dante guy and his little friend do this little disappearing trick a lot.* She reasoned, *but then again, they were the bad guys and they did it of their own free will. With Destiny gone we will have no one who can heal us if something else goes wrong...*

Jack's thoughts were interrupted by the sound of the back door to the church opening. She turned to see who it was, and recognized the man standing in the doorway. "Dad, someone's here to see you." Pastor Chad left to go talk to the guy, leaving Jack alone in the room with the unconscious Conner. He seemed to be pretty out of it, so she decided to go see how the battle was going between Axel and Dante. Carefully she took Conner's pouch of arrows away from him and slung it over her own back. She had never shot a bow and arrow before, but how hard could it be? Anyway, it was worth a try. Armed with Conner's weapons, she walked back out of the sanctuary towards the front doors, half-smiling at the newcomer who was discussing something with her father in the hallway.

The two front doors to the church were made of glass, so even before she reached them, Jack knew that something was wrong. There was no longer a battle going on outside. There was only a lifeless lump laying on the ground. Jack's eyes grew wide, fearing the worst. She screamed out his name, alerting her father and his visitor to her distress. She ran at the doors, pushing them open with her side, and did not stop running until she was right next to Axel. She fell down on her knees next to him, tears in her eyes, yelling at him to wake up. She was panicking. She didn't know what to do. She tried to shake him awake, but he just hung there, comatose in her arms. She tried to pick him up, to get him to the church, but he was much too heavy for her to carry on her own. Luckily, her father and the man he had been talking to had followed her outside. Between the two guys, they managed to get Axel back inside the church and laid him down on a pew close by to where Conner was.

"Is he...?" Jack asked, unable to finish the thought through her tears.

Chad stayed calm and checked Axel's pulse. He gave his daughter a reassuring smile. "He's still alive." Chad examined the wound in Axel's stomach. "It's not very deep. There's not even a lot of blood. I don't understand why he's passed out." Chad wore a puzzled expression as he surveyed the two unconscious men in his sanctuary. He sighed. *What have I gotten myself into??*

"Uhm, is everything alright here?"

Jack jumped when she heard the voice, having forgotten already that the man was here.

"Everything will be fine. Why don't you come back later and I can discuss this further with you?" Chad answered him, handing him the Bible that he had set down to chase after Jack. "John, chapter fifteen, right?"

"Yeah..." He said uncertainly, then, surveying the scene again, added, "Are you sure you don't want me to call an ambulance or something?" The man clearly did not want to leave. He brushed a strand of curly blonde hair out of his eyes. Jack saw him look over at her and their eyes met for just a moment. She always thought he had the most beautiful blue eyes she had ever seen. She looked away, blushing. *He's way too old for me.* She thought, *I'm only sixteen, and you're, what? Twenty? Twenty-one?* She didn't know for sure, but, in any case, she knew her father would never allow it. *Perhaps when we're older it won't seem like such a big difference.* Then she looked back down to Axel. *I wonder how old you are?* She smiled at him, relieved that he was alive, and happy that she was going to get the chance to get to know him better.

Chad ushered their visitor out the door and then came back to the room where his daughter sat, patiently waiting for her friends to awaken. Chad checked his watch. It was 2:53. He crossed his arms and gave his daughter a reprimanding look. "So much for going back to school." He tried to hold the cross look on his face, but it only lasted a few seconds before they both burst into laughter. It wasn't really that funny, but it felt good to laugh. Like cleansing away some of the horrible things that had happened. If only for a moment.

*****

Vincent stared at Jarron a moment, taking in his battered clothes, frail body, and dull senses. Sure he appeared to others as a strong, confident, man, but Vincent could see him for what he really was: a snack. He shook his head to clear it. *No! Just because I am a ... a vampire,* he despised the word, hating what he had become, *doesn't mean I have to go around meaninglessly killing people. Stop thinking about his non-existent defenses and listen to what he's saying.* He scolded himself.

"How could you possibly know Sepheroth's son?" Vincent scoffed at him, thinking that he was the simplest of all creatures. *How did I ever survive in such a state?* He wondered. His brain worked so much faster now. He could compute a thousand possibilities in a second. What could this puny human know that he hadn't already thought of?

The other human was stirring, and Vincent glanced in his direction as he heard the sound of his lungs taking in air and his eyes fluttering open. He groaned and squirmed, rustling the dirt and grass around him. Vincent rolled his eyes, annoyed. *Why must humans be so noisy?*

"Eighteen years ago I was five years old." The one called Jarron was talking again. Vincent switched his attention to him, listening inattentively. "The twins Sarah and Westley were just two years old."

Vincent sighed, his annoyance showing clearly on his face. "What does any of this have to do with Sepheroth?" He asked in a bored tone, wishing that the sluggish simpleminded boy would just answer him plainly. Who was Sepheroth's son? That's all he needed to know. No one cares about his family or how old he was or whatever other sentimental babble he was talking about.

"I'm getting to that." Jarron replied, holding up his hands in a I'll-get-to-it-in-a-minute-after-I-go-on-talking-about-all-the-junk-that-no-one-cares-about gesture. Vincent sighed again, settling in for a long story. *Maybe if I just threaten to bite him, he'll talk faster.* Vincent smiled inwardly at the thought. *Maybe I could actually bite him and then his feeble little brain could be able to actually have an intelligent conversation with me.* He paused, letting his hunger take control of his thoughts. *It has been a while since I've eaten, and it would make things a lot easier...*

"My father was out, and Mother hid with me and the twins down in our cellar. I didn't know it then, but apparently Sepheroth was attacking our city and he had gone out to fight him. Father was away all night, and when he returned the next day, he brought with him a child that had been abandoned in the woods." The human was making noises, but Vincent wasn't listening. He could smell his blood, hear it flowing through-out his body. He could see how paper-thin his skin was, and how easily he could overtake him. He would be drained of all his blood before he even knew what hit him...

"He knew that we were already struggling to survive as it was, but was unable to just leave the child to die. So instead of bringing home a deer, or something else for us to eat, he brought home Axel."

Rebecca's eyes widened in wonder. "Axel? How come he never told me?"

Hearing Rebecca's voice pulled Vincent back into the conversation. He cleared his mind, and was back in control. The boy would never know how close he was to losing his life. *You are not a monster.* Vincent told himself. But somewhere deep inside, his hunger whispered back to him, *Yes, you are...*

"He didn't know. Even I had nearly forgotten until now. My mother took him in and raised him as her own, and I was the only child who knew the truth. Sometimes I think even she forgot that he was not really her child."

He talks too much. Vincent thought. Even though he had not been paying much attention to Jarron's story, his mind was able to remember everything that he had said. He ran it over in his mind. So his father happened to find a baby that same year. It could be just a coincidence. How does he know the boy was Sepheroth's son? "That still doesn't prove that the boy is the same child that was left behind by Sepheroth." Vincent said, challenging him to prove his point.

Jarron smiled. "Axel wasn't the only thing that Father brought home that night." He paused for effect before continuing, "He also brought home a sword." Jarron grinned at the blank stares he got from both Vincent and Rebecca. "This was a very special sword. It had a jet black handle with a black dragon wrapping itself around it. A dragon with ruby red eyes. A magical sword that could inflict curses without even leaving a scratch."

Vincent's eyes grew wide with surprise. "I know that sword. It was most definitely Sepheroth's. Where is it now?"

"Father passed it down to Axel when he died. He told him it was his father's. I always wondered why he gave it to him instead of me, seeing as I was the oldest, but now that I know where it really came from, I completely understand."

Vincent took a moment to process all of this information. The boy's logic was sound, it made sense that this Axel was the one that Sepheroth had been searching for. Which brought them to their present problem: Where was Axel now?

It made sense that The Wizard should know where he was. The Wizard knew everything. What didn't make sense was why he refused to help them. Perhaps he had something to do with his disappearance. It wouldn't be the first time.

"How did you find out about the sword?" Rebecca asked curiously. She was hanging on Jarron's every word. She stared into his eyes dreamily, as if she was looking at a hero. Vincent's eyes narrowed and he felt a deep growl rising in his throat. *So the tiny human thinks he is good enough to take her from me? How could she look at that little bug with any kind of respect when she had him by her side?* Rebecca did not seem to notice Vincent's growing anger. She didn't seem to notice him at all, and that only made things worse. *Who does he think he is? He is weak, undeserving. He could be dead in a matter of seconds. I would get more fight out of a bit of dirt stuck to my shoe than this insignificant little flea...*

Jarron shut his mouth and stared at Vincent in fear. He hadn't noticed it until just now, but when Vincent was calm his eyes were a warm chocolate color, but as soon as he grew angry, they glowed red. It was terrifying. Rebecca noticed Jarron's discomfort, and, concerned, asked, "What's wrong?"

Jarron couldn't speak, his voice lost in his fear. Sairynn, who had only recently become fully awake, took one look at Vincent's face and fainted again. At long last, Rebecca looked over at him, and in one swift movement turned him towards her and brought him back to reality.

Shaking his head, Vincent regained control again and said, "I am sorry. I... I do not know what came over me. Forgive me."

Vincent, my dear, you know no one could ever come between us. Once she became a vampire, Rebecca gained the ability to project her thoughts onto others. She could choose exactly who could hear them and when. It was a talent that took a lot of time to master, but she had finally gotten the hang of it. She could also hear other's thoughts. When she wanted to. Unlike Vincent, who, on the other hand, had gained the ability to hear everyone's thoughts, all the time. It was rather annoying at times, and extremely loud. It was often hard to distinguish between what people were thinking and what was actually being said. The only people exempt from this power were other vampires. Usually. When combined with Rebecca's abilities, the two of them could have entire conversations without ever saying a word. *The way you were looking at him, I just...* Vincent sighed. *You have never looked at me that way before.*

Rebecca smiled reassuringly at him. *We will discuss this later, alright?*

Alright, Vincent reluctantly gave in.

Jarron watched in silence as Rebecca and Vincent just stared at each other. Rebecca's hands were resting on Vincent's shoulders, and she was staring intently into his eyes. The only hint of movement at all was a slight change of expression and a sigh from Vincent. He wanted to ask if everything was ok, but he couldn't build up the courage to open his mouth. Instead, he decided to check on the sleeping Sairynn. Jarron got up and walked over a few steps to where his friend lay passed out on the ground and slightly shook him. After a few moments, he regained consciousness, and his eyes fluttered open.

"Jarron!" He yelled suddenly, slapping his hand on his shoulder with a fairly strong force. "We have got to get out of here! We are in danger! I saw a vampire!"

Jarron chuckled slightly and helped Sairynn to his feet. "It's ok, calm down." He didn't want to upset him any more than he already was. "They are friendly."

Sairynn's eyes were wild with fear. He put both of his hands on Jarron's shoulders and shook him, as if he was trying to knock some sense into him. "Friendly?!" He exclaimed. "Have you gone mad? There aint no such thing as a friendly blood-sucker!"

Having finished their private conversation, Rebecca and Vincent stood, and walked over to join the other two. *Listen to me, friend.* Rebecca said, reaching out to Sairynn with her mind. *Have peace, be calm. We are not here to harm you.* Sometimes, if done right, her powers could also have a kind of hypnotizing effect. Sairynn looked horrified at first, but slowly he began to calm down. *That's it, dear. Everything is going to be just fine.* Rebecca smiled sweetly at him, and after a while he returned the smile to her.

"Now, you were saying?" Rebecca asked, turning to Jarron, whose face held a look that was something of a cross between fear and amazement. "About the sword?" She prompted.

It took him a minute to realize what she was talking about, but finally his slow human brain caught up with her. "Oh, right. So I had always thought the sword was special, but I never really knew the whole story about it until Axel disappeared. Our town had been under Sepheroth's rule for as long as I could remember, so I had just thought that it was normal. But as I talked with more and more people, they started to paint a bigger picture for me. After my father stole the sword, Sepheroth sent out soldiers daily to raid all the nearby towns looking for it. I don't know how Father hid it from them, but he managed to keep it until the day he died. Our town was raided several times before that, but they never found the sword. He gave it to Axel when he was only five years old, but of course our mother wouldn't let him actually handle it until several years later." Suddenly a new thought struck him. "Oh my gosh, do you think that is why he is gone? Could Sepheroth have somehow found out that he has the sword?"

    Before anyone could answer, Vincent suddenly cried out in pain. He fell to his knees, his hands balled up in fists against his forehead. His eyes were shut tight in obvious torment. Without any type of warning, he stood up erect, as if he was only a puppet and some unseen hand had jerked his head up and was holding him there. Suddenly, his eyes flew open, and Jarron and Sairynn both gasped when they saw that they were pure white. There was no longer an iris of any color or even a pupil. Just a blank white void.

    Four people walked away from the edge of a great forest to find a paved road and many strange looking houses. A dark black carriage flew past them, apparently propelled by some sort of magic.

    "What kind of strange steed is that?" The tallest of the group asked, staring in amazement at the thing.

    "No," said another member of the group. She was the smallest of the bunch, and had bright red hair. "They are not horses. They seem more like carts, except they drive themselves."

"Look again, sister. There are people in them." The only other girl responded, as they watched more of the strange carts go by.

The girls continued to argue until a wide-chested man spoke up for the first time and said with obvious annoyance, "Of more importance, where are we now?" The larger male rolled his light blue eyes and got no response from any of the other members of their small party.

Slowly, the group started walking down the side of the street, staring in wonder at all the new things around them.

Suddenly the red head spoke again, saying, "I think a better question may be, when are we now?"

They continued their walk down the street until they met another young man wearing a rather strange looking shirt and even odder britches. The large blue-eyed man asked him what year it was, and the blonde-haired stranger laughed. Everyone gasped when he finally told them the answer. They were indeed far, far, away from their own time. The newcomer left, still laughing, and just as he went out of view, two more people appeared. One was a man in a long black jacket, and the other a shy little girl.

These two did not just walk up on the street as the others had, but instead had just appeared there out of nowhere. That wasn't the only odd thing about the two of them either. Vincent knew them. Both of them. And one of them had tried to kill him.

One of the four also recognized one of the newcomers, and threatened to kill him, but he was not the least bit intimidated. He only laughed and said he was there to fight someone named Conner.

Conner turned out to be the tall one with brown curly hair. He balled up his fists and got into a fighting pose...

...and that was the end of Vincent's vision. He crumpled suddenly to the ground, lifeless. After a few moments, he came back to life, and told everyone what he had seen.

"I am afraid your brother really has gone where you cannot follow." Vincent said, after he'd finished telling them about his vision.

"Are you sure it was Axel?" Jarron asked, desperation creeping into his voice.

Rebecca, focusing her powers so that she could share in Vincent's vision, nodded sadly. "It was him, Jair." Then she got up and walked over to face Jarron. She reached out to touch him, and Jarron immediately jerked back away from her. "It's ok," she chuckled, "I'm just going to show you his face." Jarron's heart rate increased as she took a step closer to him. She reached out her hands towards Jarron's face, and he flinched slightly at the coldness of her skin. Rebecca placed the tips of her fingers across Jarron's forehead, and rested her thumbs on his cheeks. Then, all of a sudden Jarron's body went rigid the same way that Vincent's had, and when he opened his eyes they were white. This lasted only a few seconds, just long enough for Rebecca to share a few moments of the vision with Jarron. When Rebecca released him, Jarron fell to his knees, gasping for breath.

Vincent looked at the suffering human with little sympathy. *You are lucky.* He thought. *You get to see the future without experiencing any pain. You are so weak that the intense torture of the full vision would probably kill you.* He tried to look sympathetic as he said, "He's many years in the future, in some place I've never seen before. I'm sorry, I truly am, but you will never see your brother again."

The future?! Jarron had prepared himself for many possibilities, fearing the worst, but the thought that Axel could be stuck in the future had never crossed his mind. It was impossible! *The future.* Jarron just couldn't wrap his mind around it. *How on earth could Axel be in the future?!*

Sairynn broke down, weeping bitterly over the loss of his family. He figured that if the future was where Axel was, his family must most likely be there too. *The future.* The one place he couldn't go, *unless...* Suddenly Sairynn lifted up his head, his eyes red with tears. He looked Rebecca in the eyes and said, "Make me like you."

"What?" She asked, taken aback by his glare and sudden seriousness.

"You've done it once before." Sairynn protested, nodding in Vincent's direction. "It's the only way I'll ever find them again."

Rebecca raised an eyebrow in confusion and asked, "Find who?"

"My family disappeared the same night as Jarron's brother. It makes sense that they'd be in the same place. I will gladly wait as many years as it takes to see my wife and daughter again. Being a vampire would be a very small price to pay."

"You don't know what you are asking for." Vincent cut in, remembering with perfect clarity exactly how it felt when he had first become a vampire. "It is painful, and the immediate thirst is unbearable. No human within twenty miles would be safe." He said, glancing over at Jarron.

"Change me too." Jarron said, making up his mind. He started this journey determined to find Axel, and now that he finally knew where he was, he couldn't just give up. He was going to find him. Even if it took 1,000 years.

"Jarron, are you sure?" Rebecca asked him, shocked and concerned that he would say such a thing. "You will never be able to go back to your family again."

Jarron looked her right in the eye, a bold look of stubborn persistence on his face. He stood up straight, took a step closer and replied, "No, Rebecca, I'm not going to lose my family, I'm going to find it again."

Chapter Twelve

"Dante!" A girl's screams filled the air.

"Xion? Xion! Where are you?" Dante was running through the forest following the sound of the screams. It was a sound that was all too familiar to him. It was the sound of a loved one in pain. He knew that voice well, and he had longed to hear it for many years now, but not like this. He didn't want to see her in pain, or in danger. He only wanted her to be safe. That's all he ever wanted.

The girl screamed out again in agony. Dante could almost feel her pain. His heart was being torn apart with every second more that she suffered.

"Dante! Help me!"

It was all he could do to keep running. He had to help her. He had to save her. Sweat mixed with the tears that ran down his face as he pushed himself harder to get to her. The faster he ran, the farther away she seemed to get. Would he ever make it? He pushed the doubt aside. He had to make it. He just had to go faster, and push himself to the limits. *Faster, Dante!* He told himself, *faster!* He was tired and out of breath, but he couldn't stop. He would never stop. Not until he found her and saved her.

"Dante!"

His lungs were burning from lack of oxygen and his legs were about to give out when at long last he came to a small clearing in the woods. Finally, he had found her. He stopped, clutching his chest and gasping for air. Xion lay on the ground just a few feet away, bound and beaten. Her once beautiful black hair was mangled all around her and soaked with blood. There was so much blood. All around her, all over her, everywhere. She was trembling and helpless, weakly calling out to the only person she knew that cared. Dante fell to his knees, mostly from pure exhaustion, and crawled over to her. He looked into her emerald eyes, that were usually sparkling and full of joy, and found nothing but a dull emptiness. Was he too late? Did she even know he was here? She had a large gash in her forehead, and the blood flowed freely out of it all over Dante and the forest floor. Most of her body was cut the same way, with very little of her light brown skin left unharmed.

Suddenly, an unseen force pushed Dante back and away from Xion. Dante slowly got back on his feet and started to run back to her, but then Sepheroth was there, blocking his path. One of his minions had appeared with him, and he grabbed Dante and held him back.

"You're too late, Dante." Sepheroth laughed darkly, "She's mine now."

Just behind him Dante could see Xion stir, she used her last bit of energy to turn and look at him. She tried to lift her head so she could see him better, but she was very shaky and much too weak. "D-Dan...te" She tried to say his name one last time, but couldn't quite manage it. The last syllable was lost as she let out her final breath of air.

Sepheroth continued to laugh, "They're all mine now." He snapped his fingers and another body appeared on the ground, bloody and busted, just like Xion.

"Dante..." cried the frail body of Katara, begging him to stop her pain.

Just when he thought his heart couldn't ache any more, his pain intensified. Her small body looked so weak and frail, she was still just a child after all. She had her whole life ahead of her. Dante fought against his captor, but as much as he wanted to, he could not reach her. He glared up at the king through eyes blurred with tears. "Why are you doing this to me?" He demanded to know.

"You did this Dante. It's your fault they are dying." With another snap of his fingers, another body appeared, and then another. Conner, Axel, Destiny, Meriah, and even that pretty girl that he had met at the church. He didn't even know her name, and yet here she was, suffering, dying, because of him. There must be something he could do. There had to be some way to save them. He struggled to try to break free, tried using his magic to make himself disappear, but nothing was working. He was just as weak and helpless as the rest of them.

"Let them go! Please! I'll do anything!" Defeated, emotionally broken, and physically bound, Dante had no other options left. He begged for their lives. He knew his was over, and he didn't care. With everyone that he cared about gone, what more was there to live for? All he wanted was for them to live. For their pain to go away. At least if he was gone he couldn't hurt them anymore. He pleaded with the king to spare their lives but he only laughed, taking pleasure in Dante's distress.

"It's too late for them." The dark king growled, "And it's too late for you." Sepheroth pulled out his sword, raised it, and swung, aiming to slice Dante's head clean off his body, when suddenly Dante awoke, drenched in sweat and breathing heavily. Apparently he had screamed and woke up Katara in the next room. She rushed to his doorway, asking what was wrong.

He looked at her and smiled, and ran to hug her. "I'm so glad you're alright."

"Are you ok, Dante?" she asked, struggling to breathe in the grip of his strong arms.

"Fine, just fine," He answered, finally releasing her. "Just had a bad dream, that's all." He smiled, and turned to go back to bed.

Katara hesitated for a moment in the doorway. "Hey, Dante?" She called timidly, her voice not much more than a whisper.

He sat down on the side of his bed to face her. "Yea? What is it, Kat?"

She looked down at the ground, twisting the bottom of her nightgown in her hands. She looked so young, so scared. Dante's heart broke for her. He was sorry that he had brought her here, and gotten her into this. She was still so small. She needed a real family, a mother to take all her fears away and a father to protect her. He wasn't good enough for her. He didn't deserve her friendship. She had seen so many horrors in her young life and it was all his fault. He was sorry he brought her here, but he was never sorry that he saved her life. He needed her just as much as she needed him. With Xion gone, she was the only thing he had left to live for.

Katara stood in the doorway, silent, scared, trying to find the courage to ask Dante what she wanted to know. He smiled sweetly at her, and beckoned for her to come sit next to him on the bed. She walked over slowly, and sat by him. He smiled at her, obviously trying his best to cheer her up, and asked, "What's the matter, Kitty Kat?"

That name usually made her giggle, but not today. She looked instead as if she might burst into tears.

"Dante?" She said, her watery blue eyes looking up into his, "What's going to happen to us... if we die?"

Dante's heart dropped. That was the very question he wanted the answer to himself. What should he tell her? She was so scared, and she looked up to him. He couldn't say he didn't know. "Katara, just stay close to me, and I will protect you." He drew her into a tight hug. "When the time comes," he whispered into her hair, "Don't hesitate to use your full power." She clung to him and started to cry, and he lifted her up and held her tight the rest of the night.

*****

"Destiny!" Axel yelled, sitting up so fast in the pew that he nearly fell off of it. He looked around, disoriented, trying to remember where he was. Conner was still asleep on the next pew, a little farther down from Axel's feet. The rest of the place seemed to be empty. What was going on? Where was everyone? Then memories came rushing back to him. The fight, the king, and Destiny! He looked around frantically, shouting her name again. He got to his feet too quickly, making his head spin, forcing him to sit back down. He felt dizzy. He put his hand to his forehead and tried to steady himself.

"Dad! He's awake!"

The sound of the girl's voice made him jump, and he twisted around to see who it was. His heart leapt in his chest, expecting to see Destiny alive and alright, like the last time he had had a bad dream about her. But the woman that came running to his side was not Destiny. It was the black haired teenager that was Chad's daughter. What was her name again? For the life of him, he couldn't remember. "Where's Destiny?" He demanded.

Jack stopped in her tracks, taken aback by the gruffness in his voice. "I... I don't know." She answered truthfully. "She was here, and then all of a sudden she... wasn't."

Axel's heart dropped. It wasn't a dream. Not this time. That monster king had her. What had he said to him? He growled in anger at his annoyingly dormant brain. The memories were there, but they seemed to be all muddled and incomplete. He could remember fighting Dante, but then he was alone with the king. Where had the king come from? Where had Dante gone? Did Axel defeat him? Or was Axel himself defeated? The king spoke to him, told him his name was Sepheroth, and that he was his father. Of course Axel told him that that was quite impossible. What else had the king said? There was more but Axel's brain refused to cooperate as he tried to recall the whole conversation. The last thing he can remember seeing is Destiny struggling to break free of ropes that tied her down. How had she gotten there? He didn't know. But one thing was certain: She was in trouble. If they were going to have any hope of saving her, they would have to journey to the dark king's castle and defeat him. While searching his memories for any other clue as to what to do next, Axel remembered suddenly what The Wizard had said to him. It had been a question, and one that he had not understood in the least. However, it was the reason he agreed to go on this journey in the first place. Axel could hear The Wizard's insanely loud voice booming inside his head: *Doth Thou Not Wish To Be Reunited With Thy Father?*

Could it be? Axel wondered with a terribly sick feeling in the pit of his stomach, *Could Sepheroth really be my father?* He shuddered at the thought of it. *Then what of my mother? My brothers? My family? Are they all truly my family? Or has my whole life been a lie? I wish I could go home now and ask them...*

"Axel? Are you okay?" It was that voice again. The one of the girl whose name he could not remember. Why was she here? Where was he? Having been lost in his thoughts, the present had melted down all around him. Now, being brought back to reality, he was confused again. He looked around and remembered he was in the church. The girl stood above him, looking down on him in concern. Her father stood slightly behind her, having just entered the sanctuary only a moment ago.

"Where's Destiny?" Axel asked again, then remembering that she'd already answered that, looked around and asked, much more calmly this time, "Where's Meriah?"

The girl had a pained look on her face. She glanced to her dad, who wore a similar look of worry on his face. Then she turned back to Axel. She sat down next to him on the pew and then put her hand on his arm. "Destiny and Meriah both disappeared two days ago, right after the fight. We helped them to bring Conner in here, and then suddenly they just vanished. Destiny first, then Meriah a few seconds later. There was nothing we could do." This she said in the tone of a doctor telling the family of a patient that their loved one had just died.

"We have got to save them!" Declared Axel, standing up much too quickly again. As Axel groaned and fell back onto the pew, grumbling angrily to himself. Conner woke, muttered something about people being loud, rolled over, and fell off the pew. He hit the ground with a loud thud and was instantly awake.

"Wha-?" He sat up, a little dazed and confused, before realizing he hadn't messed with his hair yet. He frantically began trying to smooth it out, and after a while he looked up to where Jack stood giggling at him and asked: "How is my hair?" Jack told him he looked fine, and helped him to his feet. That's when he noticed that Axel had finally woken up. "Axel! You are alive!"

"Of course I am alive." Axel grumbled. Then he got a good look at Conner and raised one eyebrow in confusion. "What are you wearing?"

"Huh?" Conner said, then, looking down at himself, smiled and answered, "Oh, Pastor Chad got me this yesterday." Conner was wearing a pair of bright green pajama pants that were a bit too big on him. He had the drawstring tied tight so that they wouldn't fall down. All over the material were yellow smiley faces of different sizes. Axel had never seen anything more ridiculous in his life. "You have some too." Conner grinned and pointed to a neatly folded matching pair of pants that sat on the same pew where Axel had been knocked out.

There is no way I am wearing those. Thought Axel, glaring at the hideous pants. Then he noticed that next to the pants was a stack of clothing, also neatly folded. For Axel, there was a plain black T-shirt and blue jeans, and for Conner there was a long sleeved, button-up, red and black plaid shirt that used to belong to Pastor Chad himself, along with another pair of plain blue jeans. Axel was much broader than Chad, so he had gone out and bought him something to wear, hoping that he had guessed the right size. While he was out, he saw that the pajama pants were on sale, and so decided to pick up two pairs of those.

Axel held up the shirt, and, deciding that it wasn't too horrible, decided to go change. Conner helped him to his feet, and together they made their way to the men's bathroom. Using the sink and hand soap, they tried to clean themselves as much as possible before putting on the new clothes. The strange new material of the pants felt wrong to Axel, but it was much better than his dirty, thread-bare britches he had been wearing. Conner rolled up the sleeves of his new shirt, and looking in the mirror, decided he quite liked his new look. He left the top few buttons undone, and then he was ready to go.

When they returned to the sanctuary, Jack had brought them food, and Chad was over in front of his office talking to someone. Conner looked up and remembered his face. He was the guy with the black shirt that said "RENT" across the front that had told them what year it was. Even though he wasn't wearing that shirt now, that was how he remembered him. So, as he set down his bowl of cereal that Jack had just handed him, he smiled and waved, calling out, "Hey, Rent Guy!"

Both men looked up at Conner; Chad with a look of annoyance and "Rent Guy" with a look of confusion. Then, recognition passed across his face, and he smiled and waved back to Conner. Then, after saying something that Conner couldn't hear to Chad, the man whom Conner called Rent Guy came over to join them for breakfast, leaving Chad alone in the hallway.

Of course, everyone wanted to know what happened to Axel after the fight, so while he ate he told them everything he could remember about the king and what he had said. He finished by saying that the king was holding Destiny - *and Meriah,* he reminded himself - captive at his new castle. Even if the rest of his memory was faulty, he knew that much for sure. Destiny and Meriah were in trouble, and they needed all the help they could get.

"Oh that is grand." said Conner. Some of Axel's sarcasm seemed to be rubbing off on him. "We never even found the old one. How are we supposed to find the new one?" He knew this was a hopeless mission. Why did no one ever listen to him? The king was going to destroy everything, and there was nothing they could do about it.

Rent Guy, who still hadn't told them his real name, laughed. "Trust me guys, castles aren't very common these days." A dirty blonde curl fell into his face, and he threw his head back to get it out of his vision. He was shorter than both Axel and Conner, about five and a half feet tall. Today he wore a plain black shirt, much like the one that Axel wore, except that his had a bit of a collar and two buttons at the top that he hadn't bothered to fasten. His jeans were a much darker blue than Axel's or Conner's, and they had a rather large hole in them, exposing his left knee. "I'd be happy to come with you, if you'd like." He said, smiling as if he'd just been invited to a party. "I know the land here pretty well."

Axel and Conner both exchanged looks that clearly said: No. They really had no idea who this guy was, and they already had a navigator.

"So, do I." Jack cut in, sensing Axel and Conner's discomfort, "So that won't be necessary. But thanks."

Rent Guy turned to face her with an incredulous look on his face. "You're going on a trek through the mountains to find an evil king's castle? Don't you have school on Monday?"

Jack narrowed her eyes and crossed her arms. It was a look Axel had seen several times on Destiny. *Just what we need. Another stubborn girl. Speaking of, no one invited her to come along either.* Axel sighed. *We do need someone who knows their way around here. Maybe I can convince Pastor Chad to help us. He is a man I know I can trust. This "Rent Guy" could be working for the evil king, for all we know. What if he just wants to lead us into a trap?*

"Who said anything about mountains?" said Jack, still glaring at Rent Guy for talking down to her like a child.

He just laughed at her. "Well, there certainly aren't any castles on this side of the mountains."

"Anyway," Jack held her glare for a few moments longer before turning to Axel, "I think you guys should take it easy for a while before going after this guy."

"Jack's right." Said Conner, (*Of course!* Axel thought, *I remember now, her name is Jacquelynn!*) "If we set out now, the king would murder you. He just put you out for two days without even touching you. Imagine what he could do if he was actually trying to kill you."

Thank you Conner for having so much faith in me. Axel sighed again, then made up his mind. They had already waited long enough. What horrors had Destiny already experienced in the past two days? What if they were already too late? "No." said Axel firmly, standing up and setting down his empty bowl. He looked over at Conner. "In the same way that you have to beat Dante, I must be the one to defeat Sepheroth. I know it has to be me. I have to be the one that takes him down. Not Jack, not Conner, and certainly not you." he said, pointing to each of them in turn, Rent Guy last. "It has to be me. I do not know how I know it, or how I will do it, but I do know that I just have to believe that I can, and I will. I will avenge my father." His face grew dark with hatred as he thought about what the king had said. *So what if he really is my father? He will pay for what he has done. So what if his magic and strength is far superior ours? The child's magic alone is greater than all of ours put together, especially without Destiny and Meriah. It will be a challenge to defeat her let alone this king.* "Let's not forget about Dante, either." Axel said, turning to Conner. "You know better than I that he grows stronger and more powerful with every passing moment that he is under Sepheroth's command."

"When the darkness surrounds Dante, he will be completely lost to it." Conner agreed miserably.

"This guy is obviously much stronger than I am, with very powerful magic. I know that I stand no chance against him, but I have to try. Even if I lose, I would rather die in honor than run in shame."

"Axel," Said Jack, shifting her weight on the uncomfortable pew, "Resting before a battle isn't running in shame. It's preparing yourself so you don't fail."

"I've had two days to rest!" Axel said, indignantly. "We do not have a lot of time. By the time we find this castle, it might already be too late. We have to go now."

After several minutes of arguing, Axel finally got his way and they decided to leave to try to find the castle. When Jack was about to follow them out the door, her father stopped her. "Where do you think you're going?" he asked her suspiciously. He crossed his arms and tapped a foot at her.

"I'm just going to help them get started in the right direction, that's all." Jack said innocently, giving him her best puppy-dog face.

He raised an eyebrow and glared at her for a few minutes before sighing and finally giving in. "You better be home in time for supper, young lady." He scolded.

Jack's smile lit up her entire face as she hugged Chad and thanked him. Then she ran out the door with Axel and Conner, happy as can be.

Chapter Thirteen

Sepheroth sat silently on his throne, his plump fingers drumming the armrest in a continuous motion. He glared out across the empty throne room, contemplating what he should do next. His dark powers had once again proven stronger than even he himself realized, and now he had transported everyone to a time where there was no magic. His only hope lay in a foolish boy and a little child. He snarled at the thought. He was king. He should be mighty and powerful, but this little girl had more power in just one of her little fingers then he could obtain anywhere at all in this terrible new place. Of course, he would never let her know that. No, as far as all of his subjects were concerned, he was still just as powerful as ever. He would find a way to use his powers again. He must. The fate of his kingdom was not about to be left into the hands of a blubbering idiot and one tiny child. He would never allow it. His anger rose as he waited impatiently for Dante's return.

"Gwenneth!" He called out angrily.

A young servant girl came running in immediately from the hallway to his right leading into the kitchen area. "Y-yes, my lord?" She stammered nervously.

He turned his head slightly, so that his cold stare fastened itself on her frightened little face. He was somewhat amused at her timely appearance, but unfortunately not enough to lift his spirits any. "Get me a drink, wench, or I shall die of thirst!" He screamed the words at her, as if he thought everything bad in the world was her fault.

"Yes, my lord. Right away, sir." She turned quickly and sped back into the hallway.

Where could that damned boy be? Sepheroth thought angrily. He knew that he was here, he could sense that much. The darkness inside of him at least left him that much. He knew the girl was here too, and that she had somehow managed to keep her powers. The most likely reason for this, he assumed, was because she had been born with them, whereas he had had his powers bestowed upon him. Unable to sit still any longer, he pounced up out of his chair and started to pace the ground.

Just then, the servant girl reappeared with a tray that held a glass of red wine, along with the bottle for him to refill the cup. "Your drink, my lord."

He took no notice of the girl, nor did he offer her any thanks. Instead he simply grabbed the cup in haste, splashing some of the ruby liquid onto the rug beneath his feet. He seemed not to notice this and lifted the cup to his lips and drank almost the whole glass in several large continuous gulps. When he had finished, his eye caught the girl still standing not too far away from him and he roared, "Well what are you waiting around for?! Clean that mess you made!"

She set down the tray on the small table that sat near Sepheroth's throne and hurried away. She faintly heard the king mumble something about incompetent servants. Tears in her eyes, she raced back into the kitchen to find a rag.

The king refilled his glass several times and continued his pacing. The wine helped to calm down his temper a bit and he returned to his throne to sip it happily.

"Jacen!" The king called out the name loudly, but this time it was not in anger. When no one responded however, he began to get irritated. "Jacen!" He called louder, but there was still no response. He cursed and called again for the girl. "Where is that ruddy servant of mine? Jacen? I've been calling for him and he is not coming to my aid."

"Jacen is not here, my lord." Gwenneth answered him plainly.

His temper rising again, he got louder with every word. "I can see that you fool! Where is the bumbling idiot?"

"I do not know, sire. Only a few of us were transported here. What is it that you wish, if I may ask, my king?"

Sepheroth growled at her, saying, "Bring me something to eat."

The girl hurried away to fetch her master some food, and on her way to the kitchen, she was almost ran over by someone coming around the corner.

"Sorry, Gwen!" Dante yelled, never slowing down. He could turn here and shortcut through the kitchen servant's quarters, but that would only get him into more trouble. "Hurry, Katara! We're going to be late!" he said, turning his head slightly to make sure she was still following. He breathing heavily as he ran through the corridors of the immense castle, and the halls were long. The king was waiting. They would never make it in time. He pushed his legs to run even faster feeling the burn as his lungs struggled to get enough air. He wished desperately that he could just use his magic to get them to the throne room immediately, but the king had set up some kind of defense shield that stopped him from being able to use any of his powers inside the castle grounds. It was quite annoying, and somehow only Sepheroth's own powers were not affected. At least, that was what he told everyone. Had Dante known the truth about his master's powers he would not be half as terrified as he was now.

"Dante! Wait! We don't even have what he wants! He'll kill us!" yelled Katara, who was running as fast as she could to keep up with him. She paused, several feet behind him, catching her breath. She knew what happened when you didn't do what the master wanted, and she didn't want to die.

"He'll kill us for sure if we don't report back." Dante insisted, only stopping long enough to answer her.

"But Dante-"

"Hush! And don't forget to bow this time." said Dante, turning the final corner to end up in the main hall where the king's glorious throne sat at the far end. The hall itself was humongous. So huge that it made the giant king look tiny (and that was saying something). The light reflected off of the gold that lay in between the bricks of the walls, and glittered off his great golden crown. A dreadfully long scarlet carpet went from one end of the hall to the other. This is where Dante was now. At the far end of the mile-long blood-red carpet.

"Dante!" The carpet seemed to go on forever when there was an impatient evil king waiting for you at the other end. The fear rose up inside Dante as he ran to greet his master. This could very well be his last day on this earth. What a stupid way to die. Killed for not obeying orders. He hated obeying orders from others. What dignity was there in that? He wanted more than anything only to be free. But now, here he was, staring death in the face. Would his last moments be spent begging for mercy? He was better than that. He wanted to stand up and fight, but he knew that if he tried, it would all be over. Katara would have to witness another death of a dear friend, and for what? What good was to come of any of this? Was it really his destiny to die here, in this hall, having no good to show for it? What kind of person spends their life running around in terror just to save their own life? His life was the one thing he cared about most. It wasn't the power or the money that drove him to do whatever the will of his master was, no, it was the fear for his own life. Dante was afraid most of all of the unknown. What happened after death? Did everything just end, or does your soul move on? Did he even have a soul? Dante was most afraid of not knowing what the afterlife had in store for him, and it was for this reason that he knelt down now, gasping for breath, at the foot of his master's throne.

"Dante!" The king yelled, glaring down at him. "You have failed me for the last time!"

This was it. His life was over. He would not beg. Not in front of Katara. Slowly, he got to his feet and spoke what could very likely be his last words. "I apologize, sir. I have no excuse." He sounded braver than he felt. He winced, expecting immediate punishment, but none came. His legs felt weak and shaky. He was going to faint if the king didn't kill him soon.

Katara had fallen slightly behind and just made it to the throne. She threw herself down next to Dante, bowing before their master. Sepheroth seemed not to notice her entrance.

"If I had not stepped in, we would still have nothing. I trust you have secured our-" he cleared his throat slightly before continuing, "guests?"

"Yes, my lord. The two females have been thrown into the dungeons as you commanded." Dante said, a little hope creeping into his voice. At least he had done something right. But would it be enough?

"And the keys?" The dark king inquired, raising an eyebrow at him momentarily before returning to his usual cold glare.

"Here, sir." Dante said, taking them out of his pocket and holding them up for the king to see.

The king's expression did not change. He stared at Dante with those icy blue eyes, full of loathing and rage. He was silent for a while and the sound of Dante's heart beating thundered loudly in his ears. Dante desperately wished he knew what the king was thinking. Was he wondering how best to dispose of them? Or could he actually be considering giving them another chance? Dante figured the first option was much more likely.

Without warning, Sepheroth suddenly turned on Katara. "Did you even try to help?" He bellowed at her, making the young girl jump. She was too startled to speak at first, and the king's yelling, "Well?" did not help much.

"Y-y-yes, sir, I-"

"Even with the powers I gave you, you failed to even injure a single one of them!" He accused.

Katara held her ground, trying not to cry. Even though she had been serving the king nearly all her life, the sight of him destroying Xion had installed a new fear in her. She was shaking with terror, and still trying to stand strong. Dante envied her, wishing he wasn't such a coward. He wanted nothing more than to run away and escape this fate. Yet here was Katara, scared as can be, still holding her ground. Dante furrowed his brow, took a deep breath, and gathered up as much courage as he could muster, and stepped out in front of Katara, blocking her from the king. He may be going down today, but there was no way he was taking her with him. "She followed her orders." He said defiantly, squaring his shoulders and standing up straight, "She's still just a child. Her powers are limited." He made eye contact with the king, matching his querulous stare.

The king glared down at them in silence for what seemed like an eternity. The tension in the air was as thick as the Earth is deep. Dante couldn't believe he had made it this far. He had thought for sure that he'd be dead by now. He stood there, shielding his only remaining friend, as a last act of bravery before he moved on. The king could take away his free will and he could take away his love, but he was not taking Katara.

Dante had found Katara when she was only four years old. Someone had left her to die out in the cold. It had been bitterly cold that day, cold enough to chill the bones of normal humans, but for a fire Elemental, weather like that was deadly. She was so weak when he picked her up; her frail little body was limp in his arms. He saved her life that day, and he would give up anything, even his own life, in order to do it again. She was all that he had left.

"Very well." said the king slowly, in his deep growling voice. "I have a plan."

Dante let out a sigh of relief, relaxing his shoulders and smiling at Katara. This was unbelievable! They weren't going to die! He was actually going to give them another chance! Another chance to... To be overcome by the darkness. Dante's spirits fell. He was going to take over again. Force him to do evil and hurt people that he cared for. If only there was some way of warning Conner... He thought back to his days at the Academy. Conner, Dante, and Xion. They were inseparable. The best of friends. Xion. It hurt his heart to think of her. She had been his first and only love. Like an idiot she had followed him here, and had also been taken in by the darkness. It was all his fault. If only he'd told her to go back, told her never to come back; to go and find another love, a good husband, someone to take care of her and protect her like he only wished he could do; a good stable home, safe, and far away from the king and all those who worked for him... But, no, his heart couldn't bear to lose her, to send her away, and so he had let her stay. Dante begged the king to let her join them, and at long last he had agreed. She only had to prove herself to him.

Xion had been the last of the earth Elementals, and the king had forced him and Katara to watch as he tortured her. Guards held Dante back as he tried to run to her, tears streaming down his face as his whole world crumbled around him, his heart dying with her. He couldn't stand the pain. Her screams cut through his chest with more effectiveness than a two-edged sword. Then the moment she slumped to the floor - hardly recognizable under all the blood. The guards finally let him go and the king laughed as he desperately lifted up her lifeless body and shook it, telling her through his tears how much she meant to him; telling her she must come back to him, that he couldn't live without her by his side. Her light brown skin was covered in fresh gashes, and the top half of her body was nearly severed off from the rest of her.

    Xion's blood was now all over Dante. He looked into her face, kissed her dead lips, and held her close to him... The king then told him this was what happened when you disobeyed orders... The effect it must've had on poor Katara, seeing someone murdered like that. Showing no mercy, no respect for human life. And to have it be one of her own kind. The Elementals were a dying breed. It was very likely that Katara was the only one left in the entire world...

    "Ready yourself and Katara." said the king, standing up to glare down on them even more. "We are going to meet the mighty Axel in battle."

    Dante could feel the darkness trying to take over again. "Sir, please..." He didn't want to hurt them. He didn't want to lose control. If he could, he would join with them to beat the king. Deep down he knew that if he tried he would fail. The king would slice him down in an instant, and after all he'd done, they would never trust him anyway. He was stuck here, and would be for the rest of his life.

    Katara turned and hit him. "Shut up!" She whispered angrily, "Are you trying to get us killed?"

    "For once the child is far wiser than you, Dante." The king laughed as he waved his hand slowly in front of him, his palm out facing his minions, releasing his dark magic. At least, that was how it appeared to Dante and the others. Even though Sepheroth no longer had control of his own magic, there was one thing he could still use to overcome others. A long time ago, when he had first gotten his powers, he was also given a ring. The ring held inside it a monstrous spirit who had been given the name of Erebus. Erebus was the Shadow of Darkness, and it was that darkness that now poured into Dante, pushing out his will and leaving only Erebus. "This is your last chance. Fail me again and I will have your head!"

He tried in vain to fight it, but before long his eyes had turned dark and Dante was once again lost to the king's power. He bowed obediently to his master, waiting for orders. "Yes, my liege. What is the plan?"

Chapter Fourteen

Jarron sat down on a nearby bench, tired from another long day with no success, and began to write...

Sairynn and I travelled for many years together. The first few we spent with Rebecca and Vincent, who taught us how to use our new powers and how to fit in in the world. As the world began to change, we had no choice but to change with it. We toured beautiful places all over the world, but still have yet to find what it is that we are looking for. Over 900 years have passed now, and I can remember each and every second of them with perfect clarity.

Sairynn, it seems, has gotten the better end of this deal. Along with perfect vision, hearing, smells, and taste, he has also gained the unique ability to turn himself invisible. This is quite handy when we are trying to sneak around places, and especially so whenever we want to creep up behind a good meal.

Sairynn and I, however, tend to have very different ideas on what a good meal is.

Sairynn likes to think of himself as a kind of "Robin Hood" type hero. He likes to find people who are ruthless and deserving of death and kill them before they can hurt anyone else. He never hurt the innocent, that I know of anyway, but he does not mind feasting on human blood. This began to create a rift between him and me, and after the first hundred years or so, we decided to go our separate ways. I never saw Sairynn again, and to this day, I have no idea whether or not he ever found his family again.

I have been alone ever since. Sometimes I like to take a few odd jobs here and there, but I can never stay in the same place for very long because I don't want the people to be suspicious of me. I never age, and if I get hurt, my body heals itself almost instantaneously. If people were to see this, they would ask questions. If they found out what I really am, they'd get scared. People do crazy things when they get scared. Like burn you at the stake, or gather up an angry mob to run you out of town, or try to put a wooden stake through your heart. No, it was better to just lay low, and remain lonely.

This is a very lonely life I have chosen for myself. I only wish that I will find you someday soon. It has been so very long. Will you even remember me? I hope I haven't missed you somewhere along the way. It may seem impossible that this letter will ever reach you, but I have to do something to keep myself sane. When I take the time to sit down and write to you, it's almost like I'm not alone.

Sometimes I swear I can hear you, what you would say if you were here. But then I am always reminded of how isolated I really am.

Besides the usual super speed, perfect senses, and super strength, I have failed to acquire any special powers with this transformation. Only an unquenchable desire for a substance that utterly disgusts me. To be perfectly honest with you, I have often thought of just starving myself to end it all, but then I quickly learned that that was a very bad idea. The more thirsty you are, the harder it is to control yourself. Especially around humans. Animal blood is great to keep you alive, but it's like drinking a year old bottle of warm pop, long after all of the carbonation in the soda dissolves. It momentarily takes care of the thirst, but it is never truly enough. It grieves me to admit that my hands are not exactly clean when it comes to taking human blood. I am in no way proud of what I have done, but all that is in the past now and cannot be changed.

Anyway, I have found a new town by the name of Rittman, and I am hoping to find a place to stay for the night. I wish you the best of luck, where ever you are, and hopefully I will see you again very soon.

Your brother, Jarron.

As Jarron finished scrawling his letter, he gently folded it in half and added it to the many others that were inside his bag. As he walked down the street, he noticed a church building up ahead and decided to go have a look inside, and ask if they might know any cheap places to stay for the night.

Jarron walked up to the glass doors of the church and pulled on the handle. It was unlocked. He slowly took a few steps inside and called, "Hello? Is there anyone in here?"

An average man with dark hair and eyes walked out from one of the corridors and said, "Hello, there. My name is Pastor Chad. How may I help you?"

*****

Axel, Conner, and Jack were nearing the edge of a forest.

"Are you sure we are going the right way?" Axel asked, looking at Jack with obvious doubt.

"Well, honestly, I've never been this far away from home before." Jack answered, shrugging her shoulders.

Axel rolled his eyes. *We are never going to find this castle. We could be going in the complete opposite direction for all we know. Why couldn't the king just fight me in front of the church? Why did he have to involve Destiny and her sister? If anything happens to them it will all be my fault. I am the one the king wants. If they die... if Destiny dies... I do not know if I will ever be able to live with myself...*

"As long as we keep going east," Jack was saying, interrupting Axel's thoughts, "We should run into the mountainside, and well, what better place to hide a castle then behind a mountain, right?" She chuckled nervously and got a glare in return.

"How do you even know we are going east?" Axel demanded to know.

"Oh! I know this one! You look at the stars!" Conner chimed in suddenly, grinning widely like he was proud of himself.

"That's great, Conner," Jack said, smiling sympathetically, "But look around you. It's the middle of the day."

"Oh, right." said Conner, going silent for a while. He was thinking back to his days at the Academy where they had taught them how to navigate by using the stars. Dante and Xion had been in that class. Of course, they were in all his classes back then. He wondered where Xion was now. Was she still with Dante? Did she know he was working for an evil king? Perhaps she was working for him too. What had happened to the three friends that were inseparable in their youth? Ever since they were sent on their missions...

All of a sudden, Jack screamed as she flew backward. It was as if a giant invisible hand had slapped her away and swept her right off her feet. She lay on the ground, dumfounded and a little sore, wondering what in the world had just happened.

Conner ran to her aid, helping her up and asking if she was ok.

"I... I'm fine, I think. I was just walking, and then it was like I ran into a wall." Jack took a few cautious steps forward, her hands out in front of her, feeling for whatever unseen force had just tossed her to the floor. After only five steps, she could feel something in the air that felt like a hard, rubbery wall. Confused, she tried to push through it, walking sideways to see if she could get around it, but nothing helped. There was some kind of force field here that was blocking her out, but all she could see was air. Frustrated, she banged her fists on the ghostly blockade, praying desperately for it to break down and let her in.

The barrier, however, had no problem letting Axel through. Annoyed, he kept walking ahead of her, thinking that she was just being silly. "We do not have time for this nonsense. Keep up or you will be left behind."

"I can't!" Jack cried, tears coming to her eyes. "It-" She slammed both her fists on the imperceptible surface, "will... not... let... me... pass!" With every word, she hit the invisible wall harder, but it refused to cave.

Conner stepped back and examined the wall. Well, as best as anyone can examine an invisible wall. He walked all around Jack with a puzzled expression, and could find no reason why she shouldn't be able to pass through. *Perhaps she just needs a little help*, he thought, grabbing her hand and pushing forward on the air in front of him. He felt nothing, but he soon found that she was the only one that it wouldn't let through. Conner tried to think of where he had seen something like this before, when suddenly it struck him. "Oh! I know what this is!" He said excitedly, "It is a Shamira Fortification Spell. I learned about them back in the Academy. They repel all non-magical creatures and mirror their environment, so that you will not see whatever it is that they are protecting. It was said that all the great wizards used them to keep out any unworthy or unwanted guests. I had always thought that it was just a myth."

Jack fell to her knees, angry and tired, and wept bitterly. *I'm being repelled. Repelled! Like an insect. An unwanted pest. Just because I'm ordinary. There is absolutely nothing at all that is unique or remarkable about me, and this wall is here to prove that. So this is it, I'm stuck here, forever alone. I can't go any farther. This is the end of my journey. I will never see Axel or Conner or Destiny or Meriah again. They're going to go on without me, and I will never know if they found the castle or if they won the battle.* Jack pounded her fists on the invisible barrier in frustration once more. *And it's all because of this stupid wall!*

"That's ridiculous. I have no magic and it let me through." Axel complained.

Conner shrugged his shoulders, as if he didn't know why Axel couldn't get through. *If only you knew your true power...* He thought. *No time for that now.* What should they do? They couldn't just leave her here all alone to fend for herself. This place was dangerous. Especially if there was a giant evil king running around... "Axel, you go on ahead, I will stay with her." Conner said, kneeling down next to Jack and trying to comfort her.

"No!" Jack choked out through her tears, "You h-have t-to..." She sobbed, "Go with h-him." There was no way Axel could do this alone. Heck, he probably couldn't even do it with Conner, but they had to try, and the more help the better. Jack only wished there was something more she could do.

Conner looked up at Axel, who looked extremely irritated that they were not moving on already, and then back at Jack. He put his hand on her cheek, and looking into her eyes, he said, "We will come back for you. I promise." Before he got back up, he pulled off a ring from his right hand, and handed to her. "This is one of my most valued belongings. It was given to me when I graduated from The Academy. There is only one other like it in the entire world. This is a token of my vow to you."

"Enough with the sentimental stuff already! People could be dying as we speak!" Axel interrupted, growing more exasperated by the minute. Conner closed Jack's hand over the ring, and hugged her one last time before getting up and joining Axel on the other side of the barrier.

They had only gone a few steps when the land beneath their feet began to slant steeply downward. As they looked ahead of them, they noticed that the trees were beginning to thin and there was a rather large clearing up ahead. Just barely visible through the woods, was a large, stone, castle. Conner's heart leapt with joy. They had found it! Then immediately his happiness melted into dread. This wasn't going to be easy. There was going to be a fight here today, and he might not make it out of this alive. Still, he would follow his mission. He would protect Axel. He would not go down without a fight.

As they neared the giant castle, Axel's heart rate began to increase. This was it, possibly his final moments.

Would he die here, trying to save his friends? All the answers he was looking for lay right inside those castle doors, but was he brave enough to go and find them? Why had The Wizard sent him on this mission anyway? Could he really have known that he would end up here, in this time, fighting to save these girls he barely even knew? And yet, one of them he had come to think rather fondly of. He almost missed their back and forth banter, and the way she would roll her eyes. He liked her bright red hair, and her stunning green eyes that were always so alive with the fiery feistiness that lived inside of her. He missed her stubbornness and her magic, and the way she could transform into a tiger at will. With each step he got a little closer to the castle, and a little closer to his fate. Would he ever see her again? Would he ever hold her in his arms? Then, an even worse thought occurred to him: What if he did find her, and free her, and she chose instead to be with someone else? What if she did not return his feelings? He glanced back at Conner, his ever-faithful best friend. Would he be able to let her go? To see her with him and not feel jealousy and wrath? He shook his head to try to clear it. They would deal with all of that later when the time was right. Right now, their top priority was to find her and save her.

The castle was enormous, easily the biggest building that either of them had ever seen. It was made entirely out of stone that was held together with gold. A rather odd combination, to be sure, but to each his own. The conical spires at the tops of each of the many towers were also made of gold, as well as the great archway overtop of the main doors. The towers on either side of the main entrance doors held flags at their peaks. A great black fire-breathing dragon with red glowing eyes was pictured on the flags, and he seemed to almost come to life as the flags waved slightly in the wind.

Axel and Conner looked all around the castle for any sign of Dante or the king. They had to be ready for them, they knew they were coming. They couldn't just walk right up to the castle and get inside. That would be way too easy. They were about ten feet in front of the giant golden doors when Conner heard a familiar voice behind him.

"This is your last chance, Conner." Conner turned, and sure enough Dante appeared right behind him. His sword was drawn, but he was not in a fighting stance. "This is the final battle." Dante said, moving his sword around casually as he spoke, "Are you man enough to kill your childhood friend? This is the end, Conner. One of us must die today. I am sure even you must have figured that out by now." He finished this last statement by holding out his sword towards Conner, a sly smile on his face, daring him to make the first move.

Conner looked into his eyes, and knew that his friend was already long gone. The eyes are the windows to the soul, after all, and Dante's were pitch black. Without breaking eye contact, Conner grabbed an arrow and docked it onto his bow. "I am truly sorry, Dante." With that, he pulled back on the string, and released the arrow. The shot, no matter how well it was aimed, was just not quick enough to reach its target. Dante easily side-stepped the arrow and was not harmed in the least.

Dante laughed. "Still trying to fight with those old wooden arrows?" He shook his head, then motioned for someone to come to him. From out of the shadows came the same little girl that always followed him everywhere. Dante nodded to her, and instantly her hands were engulfed in flames. She formed a ball of fire and shot it directly at Conner, who instinctively ducked out of the way by diving for the ground. In the process, however, he dropped his bow, which is exactly what the girl had been hoping for. Her next shot didn't miss, and thankfully this time she wasn't aiming at Conner. Conner watched, horrified, as his precious bow when up in flames, rendering all of the arrows still in his pack completely useless. Slowly, he got to his feet, knowing that this truly was the end. He was out-numbered, and now he had no way to protect himself. His only regret was that he had failed to do his job. He wasn't good enough to watch over

Axel. He had failed him as a friend. His only wish now was that somehow, his death would help to strengthen Axel, and that it would by some means help him to beat the king and finally learn of his true destiny. That was all he ever wanted. It was never about him, or Dante, or anyone else. All that mattered was that Axel was ok.

As soon as Axel saw Dante, he knew that the king must not be far behind. "Sepheroth! Show yourself!" He shouted into the air. He heard his evil chuckle blowing through the wind before he saw him.

"My son, you have returned." The voice said, still unseen. Before Axel even had time to draw his sword, Sepheroth was there, his sword out, and ready to go. He drew it up high and said, "You're late. The battle has already begun." Swift as lightning his sword came down, just barely missing Axel's skull as he dodged out of the way.

"I do not care what you say!" Axel yelled as he struck out at the king, "You are not my father!"

The dark king just laughed and shook his head. He lashed out again, slicing through Axel's left arm and very nearly severing it off. Axel screamed out in agony, but continued to fight.

A few feet away, Dante was advancing towards Conner, seconds away from ending his life. "Conner, you are no match for me." He smiled maliciously, "The Master has given me ultimate power. However, I at least want a fair fight." In a turn of events that Conner never saw coming, Dante threw down his sword at his feet, and drew out its twin, waiting for Conner to get up and fight. Stunned and confused, Conner slowly rose to his feet, picking up the sword in the process. Dante's evil grin spread wider across his face as he immediately slashed out at his old friend. Dante was without a doubt much stronger and more skilled then Conner. He now wielded a gigantic double-edged sword, which, despite their obvious length and weight, he spun around effortlessly and ruthlessly toward Conner. Conner, however, was having trouble lifting the thing, let alone fighting with it. It was all he could do to block and dodge Dante's relentless attacks.

Knowing that he was fighting a losing battle, Conner decided to try another strategy. "Sepheroth has given you nothing but hatred... and pain! Can you not see it, Dante? He is only using you for his own gain." Conner tried desperately to reason with his friend; to find the person that he once knew. Somewhere, buried deep down inside, he had to still be in there. Conner knew there was no way to beat him, and if he didn't succeed Dante would be under the king's control forever. The only way to do it would be to distract him. Conner thought about how to go about this. While he was trying to formulate a plan, one of Dante's sharp blades grazed his cheek. The blood started to drip out as Conner screamed out in pain. He would have to think of something quick, and not let his guard down by thinking too hard. He decided to go with the first thing that popped into his head. A joke. "So there is a guy who walks into a bar with a giraffe." Conner said, swinging his sword up and then clashing it down on Dante's.

"What?" asked Dante, completely confused by this outrageously random statement, as Conner had hoped he would be.

"After they have had a few drinks, the giraffe passes out." Conner managed to scrape Dante's arm, and as he did so, he kicked him in the stomach. *I am making progress.* Conner thought. *I just might pull this off.* He blocked another blow from Dante and then continued, "As the man gets up to leave, the bartender calls out to him, 'Hey, you can't leave that lyin' there!'" With that, Conner managed to make a pretty deep cut into Dante's leg, and at the same time, kick his sword out of his hands. Dante, paying no attention to his fallen sword, produced his claws and continued to lash out at Conner. "The man looked up at the bartender and said, 'That's not a lion, it's a giraffe!' and walked away." Conner kicked Dante in the stomach once more, and he fell to the ground. "I'm sorry my friend," he said, raising his sword, "but there is no other way to release the bond he has on you." Conner brought down his sword and pierced it right into Dante's heart. His black eyes faded to blue as the spell was broken. Conner removed the blade from his former friend with a heavy heart.

Katara, seeing that Dante had fallen, cried out his name and ran towards him. "No!" She started to cry as she ran to help her only friend. She knelt down next to him and lifted up his hand. "Dante! Don't leave me! Please! You're the only friend I have left!" Then she looked up and saw Conner cleaning off his bloody blade. "You!" she said, her flames returning and growing larger as her anger grew. "You did this!" She screamed. The fire crawled up her arms and engulfed almost every part of her body. Dante had never seen her flames shoot so high. "I will kill you for this!"

For a second Dante felt a moment of pride. She really did care. She thought this was the end and she was doing what Dante had told her to do. She had finally learned how to release her full power... and she was going to use it to turn Conner into a pile of ash.

"Katara, no!" Dante managed to cry out weakly. He was slipping away. He could see the light at the end of the long tunnel but he wanted to resist it. He still didn't know where that tunnel led. What would happen to him once he passed through the light on the other side? He wasn't ready. He couldn't die now. He had to live so that he could find out where Xion was... That was it! He realized in that moment the reason that he was so afraid of death. It was because of Xion and how she died, right there in the throne room, right in front of his eyes. If he gave up and died, would he be giving up on his fight to find her, or would he be going to meet her in the air? Does everyone even go to the same place when you die? Dante didn't think so, because, thinking of all the millions of people that must have died since the earth was first created, that one place would be extremely crowded. In a place like that how would he ever find her? What if he got sent to a different place than her? Would there be a way to get to her, or would he be stuck where ever he was for all of eternity? Maybe when you died you would just come back as someone or something else. If this was true, Xion could be anyone, anywhere, walking around alive on this earth with him, he just didn't know it. If she didn't look like herself, how was he ever supposed to find her anyways? Dante's worst fears were that the search was already over. That the moment she died she was just gone, lost to him forever, disappeared into the air as if she'd never existed. What if there was no light at the end of the tunnel, and your spirit just died along with the rest of you? Dante couldn't bear this thought. He had to be strong. He had to fight. For Xion, for Katara, and for Conner, his renewed best friend. "He has set me free."

Seeing that Dante was still alive, Conner dropped the sword, and knelt beside him. If only Destiny were here. Conner thought, then, slapping himself for being so stupid, remembered that she was here, he just didn't know where exactly. "Dante, do you know where Destiny is? She can save you."

Slowly, Dante reached into his pocket and pulled out the dungeon keys. "Kat... show him the way..." His words faded as he slipped into unconsciousness.

Conner scooped him up into his arms as Katara grabbed the keys. Together they ran towards the castle.

Thinking that Dante was dead, Axel gained a little bit of confidence. At least they were no longer out-numbered. But where was Conner taking him? He should be staying here and joining in the fight. Two against one would give them a better chance at beating the king. He tried not to let his doubt show as he said, "You are all alone, Sepheroth. You cannot win."

The great king only laughed at him. "I do not need anyone to help me win." With that, he lunged at Axel, piercing his heart in one final, fatal blow. As Axel falls, Sepheroth's laugher grows deeper and his whole body slowly begins to grow. "Finally!" He yells triumphantly, "I have ultimate power!" He then began to transform, until at last there was no longer a man standing before the fallen Axel, but instead a giant black dragon. The power of the Dragon King had finally been released, and the world was in deep, deep, trouble.

Chapter Fifteen

When Katara and Conner finally reached the dungeons, they feared that it might already be too late for Dante. He had lost a lot of blood, and had been slipping in and out of consciousness for the past ten minutes. Conner kept trying frantically to get him to respond, but nothing helped. He would occasionally flutter his eyelids and offer a very quiet mumble, but that was it. Katara fumbled with the keys, tears blurring her eyes as she unlocked the gates and freed the girls.

Destiny and her sister both wanted to greet their friend and thank him for saving them, but he was not in the mood to chat. "No time to explain." Conner said, unusually serious, "Destiny, I need your help. Can you heal him?" He laid Dante down at her feet, and she grimaced at all of the blood.

Then, getting a good look at his face, Destiny said, "What?! You want me to save Dante? Wasn't he trying to kill you earlier?"

Conner glared at her and tried to keep his voice even. "Destiny, please."

Katara was also doing her best to look intimidating. She produced a minor fireball and held it up threateningly.

Destiny sighed and said, "Alright, already. I'll try my best." She knelt down next to Dante to survey his wounds. She gave one final look of disapproval to Conner before continuing. "I have never healed someone who was cursed before, but I heard it can be very difficult and extremely painful."

Conner nodded in understanding. "Do it."

*****

Jack had been leaning up against the solid but unseen wall, when all of a sudden it wasn't there anymore. Her head hit the hard forest floor with a soft thud, and Jack cried out in surprised pain. She stood up, and, after carefully placing Conner's ring in her pocket, slowly took a few steps forward. Nothing stopped her. The wall was gone! Jack didn't stop to wonder how or why the wall had vanished. She started to run immediately in the direction that she had seen her friends go. However, she had only gone a few steps into the unknown territory when she heard a great rustling and was suddenly overcome with shadows. Jack gasped as she looked up and saw a giant black dragon making its way towards her. She had no weapons to fight such a beast, and even if she did, the thing was easily ten times as tall as she was. Just one of its enormous claws was about as long as she was tall. Terrified, she darted behind the closest tree, hoping not to be seen. Within seconds, the great beast passed her by, leaving a trail of broken and burned trees in its wake.

Jack could now see the castle clearly, and as soon as she thought the dragon was far away enough not to notice her, she darted down the hill towards it. Something that she instantly regretted. In her haste, she tripped and fell, and ended up tumbling the rest of the way down the hill. She came to a halt at the bottom of the slope, bruised and dirty, but otherwise alright. Cursing herself for being so stupid, Jack got up and brushed herself off.

When she took a look around, the first thing that caught her eye was a lifeless lump in the middle of the field. Gasping, she ran over to it, fearing the worst. As she got closer, she saw that it was Axel, and immediately she started to cry. She shook his shoulders and called out his name, but he did not respond. He had a large bloody wound in his chest. Desperately trying to think of a way to save him, she tried giving him chest compressions, and blowing air into his lungs as she had seen her father do once before, but nothing helped. She had to face the facts. She was too late. Axel was dead and there was nothing she could do about it. All she had succeeded in doing was making herself a bloody mess. Reluctantly, she stood up and turned away from the gory scene.

I may be too late to save Axel, she thought, looking around, *but there still might be a chance for the others.* She hurried towards the castle, dreading what she might find.

*****

Dante was walking along the shores of a beautiful beach. It was a warm sunny day, with a crystal clear blue sky. A few birds sang merrily overhead, and the gentle lapping of the ocean played lazily at his feet.

He heard someone calling his name, but they sounded very far away. He turned around, but saw nothing but white sand and calm seas. Thinking he had only imagined it, he continued walking across the shore. He had no idea where he was going, but that didn't matter. He was warm and happy, and everything was right in the world.

Off in the distance he could see a figure draped in long, billowing white robes. He could not see the person's face, but he was happy to see them. He walked slowly towards the figure, and as he drew closer, he saw that it was a woman. A woman with dark skin, even darker hair, and dazzling green eyes. She smiled sweetly at him and whispered his name, and her voice traveled through the wind to him like an elegant song.

Suddenly a ripping pain went through his chest, and he opened his eyes. He was not at a beach at all. He was in the dungeons of the castle, and a red-headed girl was hovering over him. She closed her eyes and waved her hands over him. She was unleashing the full force of her healing powers, pushing everything that she possibly could to its limit. It felt like she was trying to kill him. He screamed out in pain, and instinctively tried to fight back. His chest burned inside him as the pain spread through his veins and out to every corner of his body. The relentless tormenting of his body overwhelmed him and he screamed out again, his arms flinging up to hit the girl, an automatic reaction to something that was causing him excruciating pain.

"Hold him down!" Destiny called, trying her best to continue the healing process without being hurt herself. Conner quickly caught Dante's arms and restrained him. The fight, however, was not over. Next his legs started to move, wanting to lash out and kick her away, and Meriah had to try her best to catch them and keep them out of her sister's way. Every cell in his body was telling him to lash out and stop the pain, but Destiny knew that this was good. This is how it was supposed to be. She was cleansing his blood of all the evil and the hatred that the king had placed inside of him. There was a year's worth of dark magic gummed up and sticking to his insides, and she was now ripping it all off with a single spell. Of course it hurt. These things had become a part of him; he had been living with them for so long.

Katara couldn't watch. It hurt her to see Dante in so much pain. She cried silently as each scream ripped through her heart. She wanted to help him, to ease his pain, to somehow stop his suffering, but she knew this was how it had to be. If the red-headed girl did not save him, then he would be lost forever, and that was something she just could not live with.

"There." said Destiny, dropping her arms and almost collapsing with exhaustion. "It's done."

Immediately the pain was gone. Dante stopped fighting and just lay there for a minute, letting reality sink back in. Slowly, a wide smile spread across his face. He felt wonderful; completely rejuvenated. It was the best he had ever felt in his life. All his energy had been restored, and there was no more blood oozing from any of his wounds. Sure, he still looked like hell, but he felt amazing.

"Are...you...alright?" Destiny was breathing heavily, and every muscle in her body was sore. She had put everything into saving Dante and she only hoped that it had been enough.

He sat up and grinned at her, truly happy for the first time in a very long time. "I have never felt better in my life." He said, sitting up and giving her a tight hug. Finally, for the first time since he had entered the palace gates years and years ago, finally, the old Dante was back. "Thank you."

"Can't... breathe..."

"Oh, sorry!" said Dante, letting her ago. He stood up and helped her to her feet.

"Dante!" cried Katara, wearing the biggest smile as she wrapped her arms around him. Her tears of heartache turned into tears of joy as she clung to him as tightly as she could. When she finally let him go, Dante turned to Conner.

"Welcome back, old friend." Conner smiled at him and held out his hand, which Dante took and then pulled him into a hug.

Chapter Sixteen

As Jarron talked with the pastor, Chad began to notice something very familiar about all this. He decided to go ahead and ask, "Your brother, his name, by chance, wouldn't happen to be Conner, would it? Or Axel?"

Amazed, Jarron exclaimed, "Yes! Axel is my brother! Have you seen him?" Jarron's heart leapt for joy. Could this be the moment he'd been waiting for for so long? Had he finally arrived at the right time, and the right place?

Pastor Chad laughed and invited Jarron to sit down. When they were both settled down on one of the pews in the sanctuary, Chad started to explain everything that had happened since he had found Axel, Conner, Destiny, and Meriah all sleeping on the hard ground outside the doors of the church. When he had finished his story, Chad rose and went to one of the back rooms of the church, fetching Jarron some food and clean clothes. Ever since Axel and his friends had arrived, Chad had learned to keep a few extra things handy at the church. Jarron graciously accepted everything that Chad gave him and thanked him greatly for his help.

Then he sprinted out of the front doors and practically flew towards the mountains. Today was the day. The wait was finally over. Jarron was finally going to be reunited with his long lost brother. He was so excited that he didn't care who saw him. He ran through the town, and soon found himself at the edge of a forest.

*****

Jack located the fancy golden archways and walked right up to the large double doors of the castle. She slammed both of her fists on the doors, as hard as she could, and was surprised when they opened up with ease. *That's odd*, she thought. *Why aren't the doors of the castle locked? Or guarded?* Cautiously, she took a few steps inside. She was in a large entrance hallway with a very tall ceiling. It was beautiful, but completely empty. And much too quiet. Where were all the guards? The servants? Didn't this guy have any minions at his beck and call? What about Dante? Shouldn't he be around here somewhere causing havoc?

"Conner?" She called out, her voice little more than a whisper. "Meriah? Destiny?" She looked around, but couldn't find any clues as to where her friends might be. She didn't want to be too loud, in case the king did have people watching, but she had to find her friends. She walked to the end of the long hallway, and came to another set of giant double doors. She reached out her hand to pull on the handle, when suddenly the door flew open and whacked her in the face.

A fresh stream of blood gushed from her nose, adding to the terrible mess she was already in.

"Jack? Oh my gosh, I'm so sorry!" Destiny helped her to her feet, and then, taking in all the dirt and dried blood on her, said, "What happened? Are you hurt?"

"Just my nose," Jack said dismissively, "but that's not important. Axel is dead and I just saw a giant fire-breathing dragon headed for town!"

Destiny gasped and instantly her heart began to break. "Axel is dead?" She repeated, her eyes wide in fear. *It cannot be true, it just can't!*

"I... I thought you guys knew." Jack said, quietly cursing herself for not breaking the news to them more gently.

"When we left to find Destiny and Meriah he was fighting with the king." Conner said slowly. *Axel is dead. Dead. Can it be true?* Conner sighed heavily. *This is all my fault. I should have stayed, and helped him to fight. I may have saved Dante's life by bringing him here, but I never meant to sacrifice Axel's to do so. Why didn't I stay?* Conner chided himself miserably. *Katara could have gotten Destiny by herself. Dante might have survived without my help. But now Axel is dead and there is nothing more we can do. We have lost. The king will use his new powers to take over the world. Maybe it's time we stop pretending and tell everyone the whole story. The one I was supposed to save has been lost, so what is the point of hiding it any longer? I must tell them everything. Maybe together we can come up with a plan to stop the king.*

There was a long silence as they wept for Axel, and wondered what to do next.

"That dragon is the king, Sepheroth." Dante said slowly, "It's what he's been wanting all along. To become the dragon and conquer the world."

Another long silence followed.

"We have to do something!" said Katara impatiently, breaking the serene stillness of the room. She was pacing back and forth, trying to think of a solution. It wasn't that she didn't care that the one they called Axel had died, it was just that there was a much bigger problem here. If they didn't stop Sepheroth, Axel would only be the first of many more casualties to come. "He's going to kill everyone!" Katara was trying to stay calm without much success. *If only Xion was here! She had always been the smartest of the bunch. She always knew what to do and what to say... until that day...* She shook her head to try to clear it of those terrifying memories. *Now another has died because of that horrible man. No, he didn't even deserve the title of "man", that was too nice; made* him sound almost human. No, this was nothing less than a monster. A monster that they must destroy. But how?

"She's right." Dante agreed. "We've got to do something to stop him. If for nothing else, we have to avenge Axel." There were a few murmured agreements, but no one had any real ideas.

"Oh, forget it, Dante." Conner said helplessly, after a few moments silence. *You fool*, he added in his head, *you know the prophecy. You know it's over. We have failed. There's no use pretending anymore...*

"What do you mean, 'forget it'?!" Destiny exploded. Who did this guy think he was? Wasn't he supposed to be Axel's best friend? Did he not feel the intense burn in his heart of hatred for the slime that had stolen Axel away from them? How dare he say such a thing! "Axel is dead and you expect-"

"Yes, Axel is dead." Conner cut in, strangely calm. He ignored Destiny's angry protests and turned to Dante. "Dante, the Dragon King is dead, it's time to tell them."

"Dead?!" Destiny exclaimed again, her voice echoing off the high ceilings of the castle, "What is wrong with you? Did you not hear? The king is out destroying the world as we speak!"

"Destiny, calm down." Said Dante, in his best soothing voice.

"And that's another thing!" Destiny was doing the complete opposite of calming down. Every little thing made her more upset, and every time she spoke it was a little louder. "How do we know that we can trust you? You are working for the enemy!"

Dante silently reached down into one of his deep pockets and pulled out a large silver ring. He held it up to show her, but she obviously had no idea what the significance of it was, nor did she care. Before Dante could explain, however, Jack spoke up. "Wait a minute! I know that ring!" She reached into her own pocket and pulled out the ring that Conner had given her. It was an exact match to the one that Dante held in his hand. Jack gave Conner's ring back to him and he stepped closer to Destiny, showing it to her.

All this just made Destiny angrier. Axel was dead and there was a murderous dragon on the loose. Why on earth were they standing here comparing jewelry?!?

"This ring signifies a covenant made many years ago by the people at The Academy." Conner started to explain. "A very long time ago, there was a prophecy written about the one who would be called the Dragon King."

"Yeah, yeah, Sepheroth's the Dragon King," Destiny interrupted, still frustrated, "we get it. Now what are we going to do about it?!"

"Destiny, please, let me finish." Conner said, somehow remaining uncharacteristically calm, "Sepheroth's not the Dragon King." Conner paused long enough to place his ring back in its rightful place on his finger. "Axel was."

For once, Destiny was at a loss for words. Axel... the Dragon King?? No, impossible. He was annoyed that she and her sister could transform, and Conner was petrified. If Axel was a dragon, don't you think Conner would have known about it; seen him transform before? Wait, of course he knew about it, he was talking to Dante about it now. Destiny felt a new fit of rage bubbling up inside of her. *So you have been keeping this a secret from us this whole time?* She thought, glaring at Conner, *What else have you not told us?* Conner was the one person she had no problem trusting. The one person she had actually started to care for. How could he be so deceitful? No wonder he didn't care that Axel was dead! He was working for the enemy! And he had convinced her to save his comrade! She felt like such a fool, and it only made her temper rise. "Conner! How could you do this to us?" She exclaimed, "I thought we could trust you! What else have you been keeping from us? Are you planning on turning on us, now that you've gotten rid of Axel? Are you-"

Conner raised his hands in surrender. "Destiny, I promise you I am not a traitor. I loved Axel like a brother."

This shut Destiny up, but she was still silently brooding. She crossed her arms and scowled at Conner, still unable to believe that he had been lying to them this whole time. Tired of standing, she sat down on the ground and contemplated how to best get revenge on Conner before he had the chance to throw them all to the dogs. If she was being truly honest with herself, she wasn't really quite that mad at him for not telling them about Axel. He had to have his reasons. She was mad at herself for trusting him so completely. For confiding in him and letting him see her cry. She was angry at herself for not seeing him for the fraud that he was, but most of all she hated her wicked heart for falling in love with him. She had felt something that night when they kissed. She had been thinking maybe he was the one who could change her ideas about men. The one who was different, and would stand by her side and care about her no matter what. But now she realized that he was no different from the rest. He was a liar and a thief. He had somehow managed to steal her heart away without her even noticing. And now she hated him for it.

Meriah, who had been silently listening this whole time, sat down next to her sister and tried to calm her down. Soon the rest of the party followed suit, and everyone was sitting down in the middle of the castle hallway.

"The Dragon King was supposed to be a great warrior who would rid the world of all evil." Dante said, continuing the story. "The Wizard was to pick a man whom he deemed worthy and bestow the honor upon him."

"But something went wrong and somehow the power got transported into Sepheroth instead." Conner said, "He was never meant to have so much power. The Wizard didn't want to honor him, he wanted to kill him."

"Why would The Wizard want to kill someone?" Meriah asked, deep concern etched into her face. "I always thought of him as such a good, kind-hearted, -"

"No one ever said he was 'good', Meriah." Conner cut in. He sighed. Telling this story went against everything they had learned at the Academy. They told them to keep the secret, to keep the two apart, to keep them safe. Well, to keep Axel safe at least. The power of the dragon was controlling though, it is said that in the wrong hands it consumes you and changes you so that you are nothing but the beast. Conner didn't really believe most of it though, since he had been friends with Axel pretty much all his life and he had never shown any signs of hostility or even anything the least bit beastly. Except for his short temper, he was a really great guy. Maybe that was it, the only negative effect of the powers that had been passed down to him. At least one good thing would come of this - he could now be fully honest with his friends. No more secrets, no lies. The one friend that mattered most, though, the one he was meant to protect, the one friend that had stuck by him through thick and thin, his one true best friend would now never know the truth. They had failed their mission. What did it matter now if they told the world? There was nothing left to hide. "The Wizard has always been a mystery to everyone, as he remains to this day. He was sent by the royal family to kill Sepheroth for supposed theft. They must have had some really great leverage, because The Wizard never usually does anyone favors. Very few have ever even seen him. Some say it wasn't even really The Wizard, and that's why he messed up. It is possible for The Wizard to have sent a follower, possibly even an apprentice to do his dirty work. That possibility seems more probable to me, anyway." He paused and made eye contact with Destiny. She glared at him for a moment and then looked away. He felt awful about what had happened, but to be honest she had every right to be mad at him. *I suppose this is my punishment then?* He thought wearily, *Will I never be able to find love and hold on to it?* He stared longingly at her for a moment, wishing he could take it all back, and make her see that he wasn't a bad guy. She was the first girl he had had feelings for since The Academy, and now... She hated him for sure. *I don't deserve her love anyway. I have failed my mission, and I have failed at life. I will stop the king, or I will die trying. It's all I have left.* Coming back to the present, Conner realized that everyone was staring at him expectantly. What had he been talking about? Oh, right, The Wizard...

"The Wizard, he summoned you guys, didn't he?" Dante cut in, as if reading Conner's thoughts. Conner looked relieved for the interruption. "Did you ever see him? No, of course not. To get The Wizard to actually come out, to show his face... wow." Dante cleared his throat, obviously wanting Conner to go on with the story.

"Oh, uhm, The Academy told us all about it. At least, as much of it as they knew." Conner said, but his mind was elsewhere. He couldn't focus on the past right now. Not when the present was in shambles and the future was extinct.

Dante seemed to get the message. He continued on, "This power of the dragons... it's complicated and extraordinarily rare. It's a complex kind of curse that would go into his blood and affect his very being. However, as soon as his son was born that son was given the same power. The strange part is, however, that neither of them seemed to be able to use it."

"What does any of this have to do with The Academy?" Asked Jack, who was so engrossed in their story that she had quite forgotten about anything else going on in the world around her. She was not concerned with Axel, or the dragon, or whether or not she would ever see her father again. Right now she only had eyes for the handsome blonde man with no shirt on. Yes, it did distract her somewhat that there was an abundance of dried up blood all over him, but his voice still sounded like sweet, heavenly, music in her ears.

"Well, the top student," Dante said, indicating himself proudly, "was to keep an eye on the king, Sepheroth. I followed him around and agreed to become his 'apprentice'. Claiming that I was interested in knowing his powers and all I wanted was to learn what he knew. Which was mostly truthful, so it wasn't a hard part to play, but then there was Xion..." His voice trailed off as he stared off into space, zoning out as he remembered her face, her body, her beauty, even her scent...

"Where is Xion, anyway?" Conner asked, absent-mindedly, unaware of how much that question hurt Dante.

Dante jolted, realized that he was being spoken to, and came back out of his trance. Then it dawned on him what exactly Conner had said. "I... I don't know." Dante replied. "I mean, she's gone."

Confused, Conner asked, "She just left?"

"She's dead. The king..." Katara interrupted, a little louder than she'd meant to. Her voice cracked on the last word as tears came to her eyes. "He... he..." She couldn't finish the sentence. She couldn't say it. Remembering the look on her face, the pain, the agony, the blood. There was so much blood. Then the way her empty shell of a body dropped limp to the floor as she breathed her last breath...

Instantly Conner understood. Of course, the only reason Dante would give into the darkness... It makes sense now. He lost her, he was empty, alone... Conner felt so ashamed. At the one moment when he needed him the most, he wasn't there for him. He couldn't believe it. Xion, gone. They had been close, all of them. Three peas in a pod, one might say. She was his next best friend, after Dante. It's no wonder Dante changed - went downhill like that. She had been everything to him - anyone could see that, and now she's gone... Wow... Conner had to fight back tears himself. All was quiet for a while.

"Anyway," Conner decided it was his turn to finish out the rest of the story. "It was the second highest student's job to watch the son. We were given these rings as a symbol of our promise to fulfill our duties. So, after that we parted ways and I became better friends with Axel. I was blown away when I learned it was him I had to protect. I had already known him my whole life, but I had no idea who he really was. Part of our job, however, was to not tell the story."

"Well you are certainly doing a fine job at that." Destiny said sarcastically. She still had her arms crossed, and she was staring at the floor.

Ignoring Destiny's remarks, Jack asked, "Why weren't you allowed to tell anyone?"

"Sepheroth abandoned his son when he was born," Dante answered her, "Because he didn't want anyone to take over his powers. There can only be one Dragon King. By keeping the secret, we were trying to prevent... well, this." He waved his hand around to indicate everything that had happened here.

Still overflowing with negativity, Destiny said grumpily, "That still doesn't explain why you were trying to kill Conner."

Dante hung his head, obviously not proud of the answer. "The king's power over me, it was too great... It consumed me into darkness."

Destiny rolled her eyes and continued to brood.

"Come on, guys!" Katara spoke up suddenly. She had been so quiet throughout all of this that most everyone had quite forgotten she was there. She was standing up and pacing again, unable to sit still a moment longer. "We have got to stop that monster!"

As they all stood to leave, reality kicked in. Their hero was dead. An evil dragon the size of Texas was on a rampage, and they had a tiger, a bird, a fire hazard, and a couple of swords. Sure that sounded like a lot, but when up against something so unbelievably huge, it was pretty much like trying to put out a fire with gasoline. You're only going to make him more upset.

With absolutely no plan, and even less hope, they slowly started to walk back down the hallway towards the entrance doors.

Chapter Seventeen

Dante was in the lead as they all walked in silence. When he got to the doors, he paused, taking a deep breath and letting it slowly back out. Gathering up all of his courage, he pushed open the doors and led the way out of the castle. Destiny was the last out the door, not wanting to face the fact that they were about to see the dead body of one of her dearest friends outside. *Maybe it's not too late.* Destiny thought, trying to calm herself down. *Maybe I can still heal him...*

As soon as they were outside, Jack gasped and ran to the spot where she had last seen Axel's body. "He's gone!" She cried, looking around incredulously, as if she almost expected to see him walking around. "But, but that's impossible! I saw him, I tried to help him, he was dead!"

As Jack frantically looked around for any sign of what had happened to Axel, the rest of the group just stood there, looking beaten. There were many tears shed that day.

Surveying the land around him and trying to come up with any kind of plan, Dante noticed his discarded sword on the ground, and instantly felt awful for what he had done earlier. He knew that Conner's most prized possession (besides his hair, of course) had been his bow, and he had told Katara to destroy it. He walked over to his sword, picked it up gingerly, wishing that he could take it all back. Slowly, he placed the sword back into its rightful place on his side.

So this was it. The last stand. Dante looked around at their little group, wondering what the others were thinking. He was scared to death to face Sepheroth again, but he would not show it in front of his new friends. He stood up straight and tall, glad to have both his swords back in their rightful places at his sides. He knew he was most likely not going to make it through the day, but he was not going down without a fight. He wasn't going to be remembered as a coward. If for nothing else, he would fight to avenge Xion. If anything in this life was worth dying for, she was it.

"What is that?!" Katara exclaimed suddenly, throwing her arm into the air to point at something in the sky. The rest of the group looked up and gasped. It was a dragon, but not the same one Jack had seen earlier. Sepheroth had transformed into a giant spiky black dragon, matching the picture on the flags that flew over his castle. No, this dragon was different, and yet somehow very much the same. The type of dragon was the same; the spikes on its head leading all the way down the spine to the tip of the tail; but this dragon was slightly smaller with shiny white scales that seemed to be made of pearl. The scales glittered and shone with all the colors of the rainbow as the magnificent creature soared through the sky. The area around them grew dark as the creature flew above them and its shadow covered the entire group of friends as they stood staring mesmerized up into the sky. Somehow they could tell that this creature was not monstrous, but pure. It had claws long and sharp enough to kill with a single swipe, but no one was afraid of it. They all knew that this dragon was good. This dragon was different. This dragon just might be the answer to their prayers.

Slowly the creature glided down towards them, and landed rather roughly a few feet away. It growled once, as if frustrated, and then said, "Come." It was strange and awesome to hear it speak. It sounded oddly familiar, but it was more gravelly, and more beast-like than anything they had ever heard before. The dragon motioned at them with its large head, obviously wanting them to come closer.

Dante and Conner looked at each other, and then back to the beast. "Could it be?" Conner asked, hope rising up in his voice. Dante just shrugged his shoulders and followed him as they cautiously stepped closer.

The girls, however, stayed where they were. All except Katara. She took a few steps forward, wanting to follow Dante.

Conner walked right up to the dragon's head, and touched its face, looking into its eyes. "Dante, look!" He exclaimed, "Look, it's him! The Dragon King has returned!"

Dante got down respectfully on one knee, bowing his head, and placing a closed fist over his heart. Conner took a few steps back and followed suit.

"Get on." The dragon said, lowering its head to the ground.

Dante grabbed hold of one of the dragon's spikes to help pull himself up, then placed himself in between two of the spikes on its back. He held onto the spike in front of him for support. Conner went back to the girls, and urged them to come along. Then he helped each of them up onto the dragon's back. Destiny refused his help, but was happy he was there to catch her when she fell back down. After she got settled down, Conner held out his hand to help Meriah up, but she did not take it.

"I can fly myself, thanks." She said, and within a few seconds her dress had already fallen to the ground as she soared high above them in her bird form. Dante then helped Conner up, and they were on their way.

Each person sat in between two spikes, following Dante's example. Together they all formed a single file line of five people down the creature's back. Suddenly, the dragon took off into the air, and everyone grasped the spikes in front of them and held on for dear life.

*****

Jarron wandered through the woods looking for any sign of his brother or his friends. His excellent hearing picked up the sounds of many different forest creatures, the wind, and the rustling of leaves, but no indication of Axel.

He drew in a deep breath, sniffing the air around him. The odor was overwhelming. Some smells were sweet; like the blood of the animals, or the scent of the flowers. But mostly he got a giant whiff of all the stuff he didn't want to smell... like all the "presents" that wild animals leave behind. He grimaced, and reluctantly tried again. Very faintly, if he concentrated really hard, he could tell that humans had been by here not too long ago. He had no idea if it was Axel and his friends, but it was the only clue he had. He slowly began to try to follow the very faint smell.

After some time walking through the woods, Jarron noticed a new smell. That of burning wood. It seemed to be coming from the same direction he was already headed, and it was strong enough to block out most of the other aromas.

After only a few minutes, he realized the smell was coming from a large path of ruined trees. Something very large had been through here...

Suddenly he heard a growl and looked up to see a magnificent white dragon fly overhead. He wanted very much to follow the creature. It was fascinating. After 900 years of life, not much surprised him anymore, but this was something he had never seen before. He tried not to think about it. *I can always find it later. Right now, I have to find Axel. I'm so close, I can't lose him now...*

*****

"It's over, Sepheroth!" the mighty creature growled, "Show yourself!" The dragon roared as it circled around in the sky. From this height, they should definitely be able to see a giant black dragon roaming around, but they could not find him anywhere. Suddenly, the creature they were riding let out an enormous roar that sounded like a thousand pieces of glass all shattering at once, and at first that's kind of what it looked like. Then they noticed it wasn't glass at all but ice. The dragon was shooting ice out of its mouth and all around the ground in front of him.

"Wow." said Katara, mesmerized by the wonderful display of elements before her. Granted, it wasn't her own, fire, but she had never before seen an ice elemental, and she figured this was as close as she'd ever get. This was better really, because not only did she get to see the element, but it was coming from the most beautifully shiny creature she had ever seen.

The dragon followed the path of destruction left by Sepheroth, and swooped down in the middle of the woods where it suddenly ended. The king must be hiding here somewhere. Perhaps he had transformed back into his human self to avoid detection. But how had he known they were coming? Even though he was outnumbered, Sepheroth just wasn't the type to run away from a fight. So where had he gone?

Since Meriah had left her dress far away, she stayed in her bird form and continued to fly around overhead. She scouted the surrounding areas for any sign of the king, but still saw nothing but trees and a few other woodland creatures running away in fear from the giant dragon that had just landed in their forest. The rest of the gang clumsily got down off the dragon's back. Conner instinctively reached for his bow, only to realize with great sorrow that it wasn't there. Jack was the last to get off, and her foot caught on something, sending her falling to the ground with a hard thud and a rather loud crack that could only be the sound of bones breaking. Jack cried out for help, her body racked with too much pain to be embarrassed. Destiny immediately ran back to help her.

Suddenly the king's voice filled the air surrounding them, bouncing off of all the trees and the forest floor. "What have you done?!"

Destiny ignored the voice as she tried to help Jack, but everyone else looked around in confusion, trying to locate the source of the voice. Dante pulled out one of his swords, ready to attack. The mighty dragon growled again, spewing deadly spikes of frozen water all around him.

A few seconds later, the king appeared before the creature, looking unusually small in his human form. "No! I am the Dragon King! I shall rule all! What have you done?! Why can't I transform?!"

"It's over, Sepheroth." The dragon replied in its low growling voice. "Now I must end this." He breathed out ice towards the king, who just barely managed to dodge the attack.

The king had to think fast if he was going to keep his life. "Join me, my son. We can rule this world together!"

"I would rather die here then join you!" The dragon replied.

Suddenly everything was very clear in Conner's mind. As soon as Axel had released his powers, he became The Dragon King. It was all happening just as The Academy had predicted it would. This was the moment that the king had been trying to avoid. He wanted to get rid of Axel before he realized his true potential. Now that Axel had finally unlocked his true destiny, the king was powerless. He had lost the one thing that he chose to live for. All these years he could never figure out why he was unable to transform, and when he heard of Axel's survival he suddenly knew why. There can only be one Dragon King. If the king killed Axel, then he could keep his powers forever, but now that Axel had discovered his potential, Sepheroth was left with nothing. He had lost. Which means, Conner's mission was finally over. He had succeeded. A little differently than planned, but it had worked nonetheless.

The king knew this was the end. He now had no advantage over his child. He was going to lose everything. He was moving as quickly as he could to keep from being pierced by a thousand tiny ice blades as they came flying at him from the mouth of the dragon. This wasn't fair! *He* had been given the power of the dragon. How is it that this boy was able to steal it away from him? This stupid boy that had murdered his own mother? The stress that it took to deliver the child was too much for Mira. She died just after he was born. That was the true reason why he had left the child. That is why he hated the boy so much. Not only would he grow up to one day steal his throne, but he had also stolen the only woman he had ever loved. His powers were all he had now. He had only wanted to give her the world. He knew with this power he'd be able to conquer all; to give her anything that she desired. That's all he wanted. Why did she have to die? Why did she leave him? He could buy her anything; got her the very best care, but he couldn't buy her the health and the strength that she needed to survive. It was all his fault. *Axel*. What kind of name was that anyway? Who in the world would name their child after a part on a cart? A young boy - especially one of such strength and good heritage - should have a strong and manly name like Rowan, Althalos, Hadrian, or Jim. Who ever heard of calling a child by such a name? His child, no less, with a stupid name such as that. The white dragon growled and shot more ice in the king's direction. He turned, and something off to the side caught his eye. A girl with red hair, not paying attention and tending to a fallen comrade. This was his only chance. A human shield. He wouldn't hurt one of his own. He ran over to the girl and grabbed her around her middle, threw her up over his shoulder, and walked back calmly to the center of the pit (with her kicking and screaming and pounding her fists on his back the whole time, this was a little more difficult than he had planned, but even without his magic, his strength was enough to overpower the girl and keep her right where he wanted her). He told the girl to be quiet, threw her forcefully down on the ground, pulled out his sword, and held it to her throat. "One false move and she dies!" yelled Sepheroth, a smug look on his face. He looked around at the faces full of shock and fear around him. He laughed his dark and evil laugh. He had done it! He had finally gotten the upper hand. This was the leverage he needed. Granted, he couldn't tell what expression was on the dragon's face, but his friend's faces were enough to show him that he was once again in control. "Fight me in your human form, child!"

"Axel! Don't!" Destiny cried out, but it was too late. Axel had already transformed.

Somehow he managed to appear with his clothes still intact. Destiny marveled at this for a minute, wondering where they had come from and how he did it. *His magic is far greater than anything I have ever seen! I've been able to transform for as long as I can remember, yet every time I do, I destroy my clothes and transform back completely naked. And yet he didn't have to even try. It wasn't fair.* She envied him for being able to execute such advanced magic after such a short period of time.

"Shut it, you! I've got at least three more hostages to use if you die, so don't test me!" The king yelled at her, bringing his sword closer as he glowered down upon her.

"Only three?" Destiny retorted, trying to distract the king so he would focus on her instead of the others. "There's five of us, you dimwit!" Normally, she would have just transformed and saved herself, but with his sword so close to her throat, that would only help him to impale her.

"I told you to be quiet!" The king yelled, lifting his foot and stomping it down hard, crushing her chest with it. She yelled out in pain and then coughed. She was having trouble taking in air. He kicked her face and laughed again, resuming his position with his sword aimed at her throat. Her nose was now gushing blood as she gasped for breath.

"Destiny!" Axel yelled, stepping closer to her. He wanted to stop the king, to save Destiny, but he had no weapons, nothing to fight with. He could only pray that Sepheroth was a man of his word. He had transformed, so now it was his turn to let her go. "Release her, Sepheroth! I am in my human form. Face me!"

Neither Conner nor Jack possessed any weapons either, but they both stood on either side of Axel, offering moral support if nothing else. They were all in this together. Dante stood up next to Conner, with Katara on the other side of him as they formed a row of defenses against the king. Axel looked down the row at his friends, and smiled at them. "It's over, Sepheroth. You are all alone."

Destiny's distractions were working, even if they were not helping. Sepheroth ignored Axel and continued to speak to her. "That mutt you call Dante doesn't count. Neither does the little one who follows him around. No one would care if I killed either of them. There would be no point in even threatening them. They're not worth the energy it takes to lift up my sword."

With that, Dante came charging full speed at Sepheroth, both swords raised, all of his anger flooding out and ready to kill. It was one thing for the king to insult him, but saying that Katara was worthless... That was just too far, and he was about to let that insignificant little swine know it. The king had only seconds to defend himself, and was forced to remove the blade from its threatening position and use it in defense. Destiny took this opportunity to crawl away the best she could. Axel ran to her and helped her stand.

"This is for all the years of pain!" Yelled Dante, his blades flying furiously at the king. "And this is for Xion!" He brought one of his blades around and plunged it deep into

Sepheroth's shoulder. However, while Dante was distracted by burrowing one of his swords into his enemy, Sepheroth took the chance to beat his other sword out of his hand. With one sword still in the king, and one a few feet away, Dante was left without a weapon. He wasn't about to let that slow him down. He grew out his claws and was ready to take on the king single-handedly.

The king growled, slashing his sword in front of him and just barely missing Dante's stomach. "This is the end of you!" He yelled, and then, quick as lightning, Sepheroth knocked Dante to the ground and raised up his sword to kill him.

Chapter Eighteen

"Wait!" It was the first time Katara had spoken since they had found the king. She walked fearlessly up to Sepheroth, and looked up at him, matching his glare. "Take me instead."

"Katara! What are you doing?!" Yelled Dante, who was still on the ground.

"Saving your life, you idiot!" her voice cracked, showing that inside she was truly terrified. Dante was all that she had; he was what was most important to her. Nothing else mattered. She had no family, and all of her friends stood here now, ready to die for each other. This was her time to step up and do the right thing. All her life she'd been pushed around by this man, but not anymore. This ended here. This ended now.

"No! I won't let him take you! Get away from him! Save yourself!" Dante refused to watch Katara die. She meant more to him then just about anything left in this world. At least if he died, he might be reunited with Xion. If she died, he would just be alone again, and she would be gone.

The king let out a groan as he pulled Dante's sword out of his shoulder and threw it to the side. He was not the least bit interested in killing Katara. "You, little girl, could be used further." he said, "Dante, however is useless. Now be gone and let me finish this." Sepheroth tried to push the child away with his magic, but nothing happened. Perplexed, he tried again, only to end up with the same result. *I don't understand...* He thought to himself, frustrated. *All my magic should have returned when I transformed.* He looked up at Axel with pure hatred in his eyes. *Am I really so useless now? Is this what it's like to be ordinary? No, it's not right. It's not enough. I deserve more. All I have to do is finish the boy and I'll be whole again...*

It was then that Conner had a sudden realization. "There can only be one Dragon King." He said quietly, speaking only to himself. *Of course!* Then he smacked himself on the forehead for being so dumb. "Axel, you have now inherited all of your father's powers. He has no defenses left. The sword will now work for you. It holds all kind of magical powers that could save us all! All you have to do is take it from him."

Axel looked at Conner, and then back to Sepheroth. Then he looked at his sword, being held in a threatening position and pointed right at him. He sighed. He loved his sword, but not what it had come to represent. "No." He said, shaking his head. Several gasps filled the air as everyone stared at him in confusion. "I refuse to become the monster that my father is."

While everyone was distracted by Axel's actions, Dante took this opportunity to crawl over to where Sepheroth had dropped his bloody sword. He grabbed it, and jumped to his feet.

Sepheroth - oblivious to the fact that Dante was now on his feet and holding up a bloody blade at him while slowly trying to retrieve it's twin - continued to glare at his son. "This is not over yet." He raised his sword once more, and then looked down and realized Dante was gone. He looked up just as Dante was about to grab his second sword. "I don't think so, boy!" The king growled as he bent down to pick it up.

Dante watched as the king placed his precious sword in his own scabbard, where it didn't really fit because Dante's sword was much bigger than Sepheroth's. Seeing his sword mistreated lit a whole new fire inside of him. How dare he take his sword! The coward! He can't even fight with two swords! Out of the people here, the only person skilled enough to use two swords at once was Dante, and he would not just stand by as his sword got put away by someone who would only use it if he lost his first one. His sword was better than that. She deserved to be out in the open, fighting side by side with her sister.

Unfortunately, without the darkness fueling him inside, Dante was not as good of a swordsman as he was before. Conner desperately wanted to help, but he had no weapon to fight with. Destiny could really care less what happened to Dante, since she still didn't trust him. Besides, she was too busy tending to her own wounds. Sepheroth now had the upper hand against Dante, his sword flying around and clanging together effortlessly with just one of Dante's. Perhaps if Dante had both of his swords, the battle might have turned out differently. However, that was not the case. It wasn't long before Dante's sword was thrown from his hands a second time, and the king had once more knocked him down. Fear filled Dante's eyes as the king raised his sword to deliver the final blow. Dante turned his face away and shut his eyes tight as he waited for the end.

"No!" Axel, Conner, Katara, and Jack all yelled in unison.

For the first time in a very long time, Sepheroth was startled. He paused, confused, and lowered his sword. Then he turned slightly to face Axel. "This man has tried to kill you and all of your friends. He deserves his fate. Why do you now defend him?"

"He's a good man." said Axel slowly. He was also confused. Why was Sepheroth asking him questions? Why does he care why they defend him? Didn't he just say that Dante was useless and wouldn't work as leverage?

"Good man? What kind of good man willingly tries to murder his best friend?" Sepheroth still had his sword pointed at Dante, who was looking broken and defeated as he lay on the ground, exhausted. "This is the path he's chosen, and now he must face the consequences." The king said, raising his sword once more.

"Dante is a good man!" Conner insisted. "He doesn't deserve this. His mind was clouded by the darkness that you put in him!"

Again Sepheroth paused to reply. "He chose to take the powers I offered him." He said simply.

"Liar!" Yelled Dante, some of his strength returning. He propped himself up on his elbows and glared at his former master. "You had me under your spell from the very beginning! I was only meant to spy on you. To keep you from-"

"And what were you supposed to do to me anyway?" Sepheroth interrupted, laughing at him, "A mere child fresh out of the Academy? Surely you didn't think you could take me on alone."

"He's not alone." Conner said, stepping forward. He walked over and helped Dante to his feet, and then stood next to him. Katara joined him and stood on the other side of Dante. She looked over at Conner and smiled. They may be out of weapons, but now it was her turn. She glared at the King, raised up her hands, and brought them down in flames. She was ready to fight for her friends. All her friends. Meriah flew over and landed on Conner's shoulder. Destiny realized the time had come to stand up and fight, together. As much as she distrusted Dante, she had to stand tall and support her friends. She walked over and stood next to Katara, transforming on the way into a tiger. She bared her teeth, showing off all of her pearly white daggers, all ready to go.

"It's over." said Axel, as he walked over to stand next to Destiny. He picked up Dante's discarded sword, and held it out towards his father. "You are all alone, and you have no magic."

Sepheroth looked around and realized that he was surrounded. There was no way out. He was outnumbered and powerless. What would his dear Mira say if she could see him now? At least her son was decent enough not to kill his own father. If Sepheroth had been given a chance like this, his son would be dead right now. What kind of father was he? What kind of example was he setting for his son? Was the power of the dragon really that important, to kill your own flesh and blood for it? *It was... No, it is...* but there was no way out. His measly little sword against a dragon, a tiger, fireballs, and... well the rest were more or less useless but still... He was out of options. There was only one thing left to do. The thing he should have done from the start. *I'm sorry, Mira. I've been such a fool. If we ever meet again in the next life, I hope you can forgive me, and know that I did the right thing in the end. It took 18 years for me to realize it, but I think I finally understand.* He took a deep breath, and let out a long sigh, lowering his sword. "This... is true." he said. Axel lowered his sword a bit as he looked at the genuinely sorry face of the king. Sepheroth had already lost everything. He deserved death. Why didn't they just kill him? He had been a horrible person. He had been a horrible father. "Axel, my son, the power of the darkness was over me, too."

Even in her tiger form, Destiny was still capable of rolling her eyes. "Yea, right! Why should we believe you?" Destiny growled.

"Hear him out, Des." said Axel, lowering his sword. He didn't put it away, but he no longer had it up and ready to strike.

"Honestly. I never realized it until now." He dropped his sword and grasped his shoulder in pain. He was losing a lot of blood. His voice was less beastly now; more human; more... fatherly.

"Des, help him." urged Axel.

"What?!" exclaimed Destiny, "You expect me to help the guy who put a sword to my throat and broke my nose? No way!"

"I don't blame her." Sepheroth said rather weakly. "It must have happened when I first got cursed. Now that my powers are gone, I can see things more clearly. I deserve this. I deserve to die for all that I've done." He coughed. The entire left side of his shirt was stained with blood, and it had been steadily dripping ever since he pulled out the blade. "Oh, I believe this is yours." He got out Dante's sword and gently handed it to him. Dante couldn't believe it. This was the same man who had ruthlessly tortured him for years, and now he was returning his sword? Was this some kind of sick joke? Or could this monster actually be sincere?

"Destiny, come on!" Axel grabbed the sword and gave it back to Dante. Then he turned to face Destiny. "Are you really going to just watch him die? Destiny, that's my father. If for nothing else, do it for me, Des. Save the only family I've got left."

Destiny sighed and rolled her eyes at him. "Look, I couldn't even if I wanted to. I... I destroyed my dress again." She said, looking away from him.

Meriah flew down and picked up the biggest scrap of Destiny's dress in her talons and brought it to her sister. Axel once again held out his rope belt, and Destiny transformed and grabbed it quickly away from him to tie up her dress. Axel gave her his best puppy dog face and she continued to give him her typical glare. "Oh, ok fine! But don't blame me when he turns on you!" She went over to the king and glared up into his eyes. She lifted up her hands and started the healing process. The king yelled out in pain.

"What the hell are you trying to do to me?!" He yelled, backing away from her.

"Sit down and shut up!" Destiny said impatiently, "You've got, what," She looked him up and down, guessing his age, "Forty years of black magic curse on you? It's going to hurt a bit!" Reluctantly, the king sat down. "Take your shirt off so I can see what I'm doing!" Destiny commanded. Surprisingly, the king obeyed her. However, when she started to try to heal him again, he yelled out and rolled away from her. "Help please!" Destiny demanded, looking over her shoulder at the others. Axel, Conner, Jack, and Dante all helped to hold the king down while Destiny got to work. A few minutes later, she was done, and the only sign that there ever was a wound was the bloody shirt laying on the ground next to the king.

"Thank you, child." Sepheroth said. Destiny turned around and crossed her arms, refusing to acknowledge him. For a moment the thought of betraying them, taking the girl hostage once more, and trying one last time, crossed his mind, but he dismissed it. He was old. He had lived his life. He had gained all the power and wealth he wanted, and for what? Just to end up here, alone, worthless, and defeated. No, it was over. It was time to move on. The king ignored the red-headed girl and turned to face his son. "Axel. You are truly the Dragon King. Take my crown as a symbol of me passing down my kingdom to you. Everything that I had is now yours." With that, he took the golden crown off of his own head and placed it on Axel. "I am sorry for the way I have treated you. You are a brave young man, and worthy to wear this crown. May you have a happy life and rule for many years." Sepheroth bowed slightly to his son, then turned and disappeared.

"No magic, huh?" Destiny sneered, watching the king vanish. "He realizes that nobody 'rules' in this world, right? This is a completely different time then where we're from!"

"She's got a point. How do you guys plan on getting back to your own time?" asked Jack.

There was a minute or two of silence before Axel answered, "We don't. We will stay here and protect this world from all evil."

"But where will we stay?" asked Meriah. Sure the church had let them stay for a while, but surly they wouldn't want them moving in as permanent house guests. Perhaps the pastor might know of somewhere they could go.

"We will stay in the new castle." Axel answered, then the turned to Destiny, who was still standing there looking angry with her arms crossed. "What do you say, Des, are you with us?"

Destiny sighed, and turned to face Axel with her arms still crossed. "Alright." She said reluctantly. "But first we've got to do some redecorating. That gold all over the place looks horrible!" The group laughed.

Axel smiled at Destiny, and pulled her in close to him. "I'm just glad you're safe." He whispered into her hair. She looked up into his eyes, and Axel had a very fierce desire to kiss her. Reluctantly, he found the strength to resist. She wasn't ready. If she wanted to be with him, it would have to be on her own terms. He couldn't force it.

Just as they all turned to leave, they ran into another familiar face.

The newcomer just stood there, eyes wide, his long, dark brown hair flowing gracefully behind him in the wind. His eyes locked with Axel's, and then began to water. "It really is you."

Axel stared at the man in disbelief. "Jarron?"

Jarron ran and hugged his brother, and everything was once again right in the world.

About the Author:

Katimeana was born on November 15th, 1989. She grew up in the small town of Apple Creek, Ohio, and currently lives in Tennessee. In high school, she loved acting and participated in all of the plays and musicals that her school put on. In 2011 she moved to Tennessee to get a new start on life. She loves to draw, write, and act. She is not currently married, and has no children.

Want more?
Don't miss The Dragon King II: The Shape-Shifting Master.
Coming soon!

*****

...Chapter One...

A man stood in the shadows, silently watching everything that happened in front of the church with great interest. He wore a black shirt and blue jeans, and a black jacket with a hood. It was hot outside, and he was sweating, but he kept the hood up to hide his face. He didn't want to be noticed. He watched the fight progress, the blood get spilt, and the girls run to help.

This man was young, barely 20 years old, but he had been through a lot in his life. He had seen horrible macabre things, fascinating events, and wondrous marvels. Not much surprised him anymore. That is, until he saw the power unleashed by the little girl.

The flames shooting from her hands were simply beautiful. The adept way she formed the flames into spheres before throwing them at her assailants was the most magnificent display of Elemental power that he had ever seen. He had thought the Elementals were extinct, or very close to it, and yet here was one desolate specimen showing off her abilities for all to see.

Now this man was a collector of unique things. At least, that's what he told people. He was more a collector of strange and wonderful people. He was building an army of sorts, and every single soldier had their own exclusive abilities. An Elemental was something that he had not yet obtained.

He decided that he must have this girl. She was priceless and would be useful to him later. He planned to follow her until she was alone, and then snatch her up, forcing her to work under his orders.

At long last, the battle came to an end as the blonde man and the girl disappeared as suddenly as they had come.

The hooded man let out a curse. How was he to ever find the young Elemental if she could vanish at will? Then he noticed the rest of the party running inside the church to assist their fallen friend.

Thinking fast, the man lowered his hood and unzipped his jacket, wanting to appear more friendly. Using a bit of his own magic, he conjured up a rugged old Bible, intending to walk inside and pretend to need help understanding something. While inside he would *just happen* to see the people who had just been out here fighting, and perhaps *accidentally* overhear some of their conversation. These people were obviously enemies of the child, but they might know more about her. Perhaps even where to find her.

Then the stranger realized the man with short brown hair and brilliant blue eyes who had been fighting the central battle with the man in the long black jacket had stayed behind, sword still drawn, not believing that the man and girl were really gone for good.

The observer let out a sigh along with another muttered curse. This complicated his plan. He thought a moment and then smacked his palm to his forehead as he realized how stupid he was. This wasn't the only door to the church. Laughing softly to himself at his own weak-mindedness, he decided to simply go around the building to the back door. Before turning the corner, he discarded his jacket on the ground, thinking he would look foolish carrying it around on such a warm day. Then after waiting a while to not seem too suspicious, he walked boldly up to the back door of the church.

He had been in this particular church several times before. He was somewhat of a regular, when he wasn't too busy out doing whatever he wanted. He came only because he thought it was the right thing to do. He knew a lot of what he did was sinful, and for this he felt guilty. So perhaps if he showed up every once in a while to church, the good guy upstairs might not be too hard on him when his time came. He was, after all, a forgiving god, right? So he figured he could get away with just about anything as long as he went to church and repented of his sins the following Sunday.

As he opened the door, the first person he saw was a young girl of about 16, with jet black hair and startlingly blue eyes. She was quite beautiful in her own right, even if she was a few years younger than him. "Dad! There's someone here to see you." She said, looking up and smiling slightly. He recognized her as the pastor's daughter. *What was her name again? Jada? Janice?* He couldn't remember. The girl's father came to greet him, and so he was forced to walk away into the next room where his office was. The blonde man opened his bible randomly and pretended to be very interested in a certain section of text. In reality, he was straining his ears to try to hear whatever else might be going on in the sanctuary. Thankfully he didn't have to wait long. They had just made it to the end of the hallway and were about to enter the office when they heard the terrified scream of the girl. They both turned around and started back the other way to see what was the matter. They saw the girl push through the front doors and run outside, and so they decided to follow her.

Once outside, she kept running until she was right next to a man who was passed out on the ground. The blonde man recognized him as the guy who had stayed outside earlier after the battle. The girl fell to her knees beside him and started to cry. She tried to pick him up herself, but he was a rather large man, and she was just a slender little girl. Keeping up the charade, the blonde man showed concern for her fallen friend and helped Chad to bring him back into the church. They took him back to the sanctuary and laid him down on a pew close by to another unconscious man. The girl was still in tears as she tried to ask her father if the man was going to be okay.

Chad checked the guy's pulse and tried to reassure his daughter that everything was going to be fine. Wanting to press them for more information, but not wanting to be too obvious about it, the blonde man asked, "Uhm, is everything alright here?"

The girl jumped when he spoke as if he'd scared her. He held back a grin, trying to still look concerned. *If only she knew what I was truly capable of... Then she'd have a real reason to be scared.*

"Everything will be fine." Chad answered him, "Why don't you come back later and I can discuss this further with you." He picked up the bible that he had discarded when they ran after the girl. "John, chapter fifteen, right?"

"Yeah," The blonde man hesitated, not wanting to leave. He had come so far and still he had nothing. Absolutely no information. "Are you sure you don't want me to call an ambulance or something?" He asked hopefully. Chad insisted that they were fine and ushered the blonde man back outside. *Damn!* he thought as Chad closed the door behind him. *I'm going to have to take you up on that offer, Chad. I **will** be back, and we **will** talk more later.*

When the blonde man returned the next day, he was delighted to see that the mysterious men were still there, and they were no longer knocked out. So he wouldn't seem suspicious, he sought out Chad and tried to remember what passage they had been talking about the day before. After only a few minutes he heard a voice call out, "Hey, Rent Guy!" and looked over to see a tall, skinny man with wavy brown hair waving at him and wearing a big stupid grin. Realizing he must've meant him, he returned his wave and smiled back at him. *Rent Guy? Why would he call me...* The blonde man tried to think of a reason for such an odd nickname when suddenly it dawned on him. *Wait a minute...* he thought, looking at the stranger's face again, *Oh, that's right! I thought he looked familiar!* About a week ago he had seen these guys walking down the street, looking like crap, and smelling like it too, to be honest, and they had asked him what year it was. He hadn't thought much of it, heck, he'd almost forgotten about it until now. *This could very much work out in my favor. If they already trust me it should be a piece of cake to get them to spill their guts and tell me everything they know about the fire girl... I just have to be patient. The day will come. The end reward will be worth it.*

"Do you mind if I go say hello?" The blonde man asked, not wanting to be rude.

Chad looked as if he were slightly annoyed, but he allowed the man to leave. The blonde man joined everyone else in the sanctuary just as the larger of the two man began to tell his story.

The blonde man listened to their conversation with great interest. They were setting off to find a castle. A castle that held within its walls the last of the Elementals. Even if they didn't want him to come along, he could easily follow them in the shadows. He tried not to show how eager he was to tag along. The pastor's daughter wanted them to stay, rest. It didn't matter much to him when they left, so long as they found their way. The young Elemental would soon be his, and this lethargic bunch of morons would lead him right to her! His plan was working quite beautifully indeed.

He offered to go with them, as a guide, but that clearly made them uncomfortable. No matter; he had already gotten the information he needed so it no longer mattered whether or not they liked him. Chad's daughter, *damn it, what is her name?!*, explained that she was going to be their guide, so his joining them would be unnecessary. He looked at her carefully done makeup and perfect nails and couldn't help but laugh. "*You're* going on a trek through the mountains to find an evil king's castle?" he asked, grinning at her, "Don't you have school on Monday?" She obviously didn't like his joke. She crossed her arms, glaring at him. "Who said anything about mountains?"

The blonde man laughed. This girl wasn't half bad, he kind of liked her. "Well, there certainly aren't any castles on this side of the mountains."

The girl just continued to glare at him for a few moments before turning to the larger of the two men and saying, "Anyway, I think you guys should take it easy for a while before going after this guy."

"Jack's right." The tall skinny one added.

That's it! The blonde man mused, *Jacquelynn! I knew it started with a "J"...* They argued for a few minutes on whether or not they should leave now or wait. The blonde man seemed rather forgotten, so he decided to head out and wait for them to leave so he could follow them. They didn't even seem to notice when he left. So he wouldn't look suspicious, he stopped by Chad's office on the way out to grab his Bible and say goodbye. He left out the front doors, and walked across the paved parking lot to the grass on the other side. There weren't very many places to hide here. There was a house right next door that would probably see him no matter where he went. How could he wait around and watch the church without looking like he was hanging around and watching the church?

Just then he heard movement behind him. Quickly, he ducked behind a tree in the neighbor's back yard. If they were to look out their window, or come outside for any reason, he'd be caught. He listened as the doors to the church opened and heard people shuffling out. He wanted very badly to turn around and look to see who it was, but with some effort he resisted. He heard voices, and knew that the large man had gotten his way and they were starting out now to look for the castle.

I should just go myself, he thought, *I can probably find it faster by myself.* He paused, listening to the footfalls of the people leaving the church. It seemed Jacquelynn had somehow convinced her father to let her tag along. The three of them were discussing which direction they should go, and the horrors they might find when they got there. Well, if there is a great evil king waiting there, and he is as powerful as they say, maybe it's best to let them take care of him first and then take the girl. Or perhaps take her while they are distracting the king. Either way, he decided, it is better to let them go first, if only to see what I'm up against. Maybe the girl would come willingly. He smiled a mischievous grin. That would certainly make things a lot easier. He chanced a glance around the tree. Jack was leading the group away from the church, following the sidewalk down the road towards Main Street.

Carefully, the blonde man creeped out from behind the tree. The three travelers were only interested in where they were going, not what they were leaving behind. Not a one of them was looking back in his direction. He was safe, for now. He casually started to walk down the sidewalk, several feet behind them. He tried to appear as if he were just taking a stroll, gazing around and taking in the sunshine. It really was a beautiful day out. Not too hot, a nice breeze, puffy white clouds in the sky... He couldn't have asked for a better day. He listened to the birds sing merrily as he hummed a showtune to himself, hands in his pockets, nonchalantly and inconspicuously following Axel, Conner, and Jacquelynn. The sound of his footsteps and humming were drowned out by the cars zooming by, and the general noisiness of the city around him. No one would notice an ordinary boy walking around on a day like today. In fact, he saw several other people outside and enjoying a walk in the sun just like he was. He blended in perfectly.

    The mysterious man followed the sidewalk across the street, so that he was now across the street from them as they turned left and continued down Main Street. He looked up and saw the eastern mountains in the distance. This was going to be a long journey. He may as well enjoy it. He stopped at a little ice cream shop and bought a large chocolate cone. By the time he came back out, he had lost sight of the three travelers, but he was not too worried. He knew which direction they were going and what they were looking for. For now, that was enough. He walked leisurely down the side walk, licking his ice cream and humming a song called "Dancing Through Life".

The Dragon King © Katimeana Keloy

All rights reserved.

ISBN: 978-1-329-89237-8